Lessons From the Vault:
7 practices to create reality and live YOUR destiny

by Saber Fatnassi

Digital Copy ISBN: 978-1-944667-01-6

Paperback Copy ISBN: 978-1-944667-00-9

Library of Congress Control Number: 2015921443

SaberWaves Coaching
4196 Merchant PLZ
Suite #355
Lake Ridge, VA 22192
www.SaberWaves.com
Support@SaberWaves.com

Acknowledgements

To my creator,
Thank you for breathing life into my soul.

To my family, friends, and teachers
Your existence in my life is paramount. I am forever grateful for
every thought you planted in my mind.

To anyone who crossed my path
Thank you for coloring my life with your presence.

To my book production team
Conna Craig, Tina Ofner and Nada Orlic
Thank you for your valuable contribution. You empowered me to
bring my thoughts to life.

Dedication

Dear reader,

Welcome, and thank you for embarking on this journey.

I have long dreamed of the time that I connect and share with you these life lessons. Lessons that will positively impact your approach to the way you pursue your journey. Pillars that will strengthen the structure of your life. Practices that will empower you today to begin achieving your goals.

Here you will find many proven success strategies. You will learn numerous success coaching techniques. You will also find stories that will connect with you no matter how different your life circumstances may be. I invite you to start from the beginning, reflect as much as you desire, and I will see you toward the end for more gifts, giveaways and workbooks.

Thank you for your persistence and commitment to create reality and live your destiny. Please remember:

Like fingerprints, you are unique in this universe.
Make your presence legendary.

The Author

- Saber Fatnassi -

Contents

Was It Worth It?

As mountains were once a granule, reality was once a dream.

N.: Tell me, how did you lose sight of why you did what you did? The sacrifices. Leaving valuables behind. The things that really mattered. The aspects of life that you've always loved, cherished, respected and held up, far from the reach of doubt. How did you lose yourself?

Maximus: I am not sure if I would call it losing... It was an assessment that was appropriate at the time based on the available information, so...

N.: Excuse my interruption. Was it an assessment or more of an assumption?

Maximus: What made you ask that question? I believe the difference between the two is clear.

N.: I see. How do you define each?

Maximus: An assessment is based on analysis of data and information at the time of decision-making. An assumption, on the other hand, is a subjective view of the unknown that could be accurate or not.

N.: Beautifully stated. Thank you for clarifying. Let's go back, please, to your explanation.

Maximus: Based on what I knew back then, based on what I wanted to accomplish and based on my priorities, I made some life decisions—decisions that shaped the way I live my life today.

N.: What did you know back then?

Maximus: I don't think I can answer that question before I talk about what I thought I wanted to accomplish back then.

N.: Would you please elaborate?

Maximus: This was at least 40 years ago. My dreams reflected my age, my knowledge and my environment with all of its fundamental challenges—financial, spiritual, relationship, physical, personal...

N.: I sense some doubt. Some regret. How accurate is my assessment?

Maximus: I'm not sure if doubt and regret are the appropriate descriptors. I would say reevaluation. I constantly evaluate situations to ensure I am still on track and that whatever I am pursuing is worth the investment. *Time is the highest investment currency*, in my opinion.

N.: Thank you for this insight. It is a beautiful life philosophy. What have you found, so far, from your continuous evaluation?

Maximus gave a long stare into an empty space, followed by a bow of his head and a long sigh. Silence took over for a couple of minutes, and then he heard the soft and caring tone.

N.: You are in a safe haven. You may share whatever you feel is appropriate. This conversation is for you and only you. You are in control of the outcome and I support you in any choice you make.

Maximus: Thank you for your comforting words. I just needed to gather my thoughts and shake off the emotions.

N.: Shake off the emotions—what makes you do that?

Maximus: I keep trying that but I don't seem to succeed most of the time. I try to drive logic into my decisions. I don't think I have made pure, emotionless decisions so far.

N.: How does that truly make you feel?

Maximus: I'm okay with it. I know that we are generally emotion-based creatures. Logic and emotions are not necessarily an easy combination.

N.: Absolutely. Very well understood. So you're saying that emotions are the actual drivers of moving a person from one situation to another. How does this resonate with you?

Maximus: I hope my emotions have not led me to where I don't want to be. I am a grateful person; at the same time I am a dreamer and an overachiever. I don't know how to dream small dreams. I have tried, my entire life, to dream practically. I would succeed for few seconds and all of a sudden, I envision myself dancing among the stars, swimming with the clouds, cruising through the sky and no horizon ahead of me. Just an open invitation into space, calling my name to proceed. Sometimes I even feel drawn to a black hole—except I don't mind living in this one.

N.: What kind of emotions does this black hole bring to you?

Maximus: Limitless. Free. Happy.

N.: How related are all these feelings to the dreams you had 40 years ago, and you have been doubting as you mentioned earlier?

Maximus: I believe those were what I wanted to achieve in my life and thus I made the decisions back then to reach my goals.

N.: How is it that your feelings today were your goals that you wanted to achieve 40 years ago?"

Maximus: I have always dreamt big dreams. It never took me more effort to dream bigger dreams than to dream smaller ones. It was quite the opposite. I have always felt energized, determined, clear, empowered and accomplished. I would swim in my own dreams everywhere and any time, in class, doing homework, reading anything, listening to any stream of music. I would lose myself to my dreams to the point where I would literally forget where I was, miss my bus stop, forget about my homework, not really see what I was reading or hear what I was listening to. I would be in my own world. I loved it. It made all my senses feel alive. I had a strange, yet strong, feeling that things would happen. While I knew, practically, that these were only dreams, I had some kind of conviction that I would achieve them one day the same way I envisioned them. I even wondered how it was possible for me to feel, and even smell, in my daydreams. They were so vivid that I wanted to make them happen. I always had hope. Even at times when I declared, "There is no hope!" I still had a rising voice, deep in my soul, opposing me. The voice always said that there is hope as long as I am willing to commit to switch my circumstances around and design my life the way I saw it. And because I wanted to be limitless, free and happy, I started searching for what I needed to do to achieve my goals. Yes, they became my goals. That's how searching for data and information started back then.

N.: Please don't stop. What happens next?

Maximus: What are you trying to get out of this?

N.: Nothing for me, really. I hope you don't deny yourself the chance of connecting with yourself. It is, by far, the best and most nourishing experience you can reward yourself with. That's only if you want it, of course. I am only here as your sounding board. You are the star here, the dreamer, the overachiever, the creator of your thoughts and your entire destiny. I love witnessing this. It is what I do.

Maximus: Why do you insist on playing on my emotions?

N.: Because you are a phenomenal power of emotions.

Maximus: What do you mean?

N.: What you have shared with me so far is filled with nothing but dreams, big dreams, happiness, freedom, success and confidence... Feelings that we all need in order to survive and thrive.

Maximus: "We" all? Are you one of us?

N.: How do you feel about going back to focusing on you, the dreamer?

Maximus: Fair enough. I think you have been good so far and I can give you a break.

N.: The feeling is mutual and I can't wait to hear more from you.

Maximus stood up by the window as the sunshine touched his olive skin. He stretched his tall, firm body as he reached into his pants pockets with both hands. He stared for a long while as if transported to a time in space—a time only he knew about.

Maximus: Perfection... Triumph... Excellence ... Exceptionalism... Distinguishment... Success. What do they mean to you?

N.: Beautiful words. What do they mean to you?

Maximus: I have always dreamed of triumph. I have always strived for perfection, respected excellence, admired exceptionalism, encouraged distinguishment, and lived for success.

N.: Where did all of that come from?

Maximus: That's how I grew up. From the first moment of realization in my life I learned that excelling in everything that I chose in life was the way to go. I learned that if I was going to do something, I might as well do it right—be the best at it or choose something else.

N.: The best compared to what or whom?

Maximus: That is the beauty of it. It was not a competition. Rather, it was about exceeding the norm and bypassing the status quo. It was similar to what we call today "going the extra mile," except that the call was for *going extra without the limit of a mile*.

N.: Wow... What an energized smile I see on your face as you talk about this. It must have brought phenomenal memories.

Maximus: Indeed. I learned tremendously from my mother and certain events, as large or small as they may seem. I remember how my mother committed her entire life to give my siblings and me the best life possible, while she had unlimited challenges that could have discouraged her from continuing. I recall this silly incident of my white jeans and shirt that taught me quite a bit. Growing up I had limited financial resources, yet I was the best-dressed kid at school, the best groomed among my peers, the best student in my school—and the most humble! I had a pair of white jeans that I loved. So my mother taught me, when I was six years old, that white clothes needed extra care when worn; therefore, I had to watch where to sit, where to step, and how to eat when I wore them. She also taught me that wrinkled clothes are a sign of careless people and I am far from that, so she taught me how to iron my clothes if I ever needed something to wear and she was out of the house making a living.

N.: Sounds like a tiny, yet empowering lesson. I am worried about your voice though. What's on your mind?

Maximus: I just hope I am able to do for my mother a fraction of what she did for me. I am not sure if I will ever be able to sacrifice for her what she sacrificed for me. I am blessed to have the mother I have and the people who taught me invaluable life lessons. I am grateful.

N.: What a beautiful matter to be grateful for. How have others impacted your life?

Maximus: They were all around me: my grandmother, my grandfather, my uncles, my teachers, even my Boy Scout leaders. It was the theme and it was the right one for me. Therefore, I am grateful to all of them for as long as I live. They taught me without expecting anything in return. They taught me to become the best I aspire to be, and more.

N.: How did all of them commit to teach you the same thing? Besides your family, were the others connected somehow? Did they have some sort of agreement?

Maximus: It's a valid question. As you know by now, I grew up financially humble, and my bigger environment was an enlarged picture of my smaller environment. This meant that my larger family, my neighbors, my friends, my teachers and even my Boy Scout leaders shared that same environment. You see, when necessity is all around you, you learn to live with what you have and consider what you don't have as "accessories." You also learn that you have two choices: either settle or work to improve the situation. The people who made a difference in my life were not settling. They taught me that life does not hand me anything until I prove that I deserve it. So it was all up to me. Since everyone shared the same circumstances, they had an unwritten contract on how to impact each other's lives. It was an imposed contract that we all learned to make work for us. You see, life circumstance and reality are all a matter of perspective. We *choose* how we see life circumstances. You must be thinking it's a dreamer's perspective.

N.: It is a beautiful perspective, I guess...

Maximus: It is what makes the difference between normal and excellent and loser and winner.

N.: You're the boss.

Maximus: Thank you for your confirmation. We seem to connect at a certain level, after all.

N.: I am honored. I think this explains "dreaming big." So my question is how big?

Maximus: Haha... You know when you are there. You see, dreaming is a blessing. A dream is the only constant conduit we can create between our present and our future. A dream is free, powerful, private, accessible, limitless and flexible and requires no extra energy. *A dream is free yet priceless, powerful yet dangerous, private yet universal, accessible yet a commodity*; it requires no extra energy yet energizes the world every day. It is limitless yet limiting, flexible yet binding. Your dream is the architect of your future.

N.: Wow... easy, pal. You speak of dreaming as if it was the only requirement for everyone to reach the life they desire.

Maximus: A dream is the soul of what everyone desires. Through dreaming we can see what we desire to have without asking permission from anyone. Our future happens as soon as we start dreaming. Dreams create new paths in our brains. Neurology scientists have proven that the persistence of dreaming the same dream creates new neurons that will condition the brain to achieve the new reality, the future. The brain will work to bridge the gap between the current state and the new reality state.

A dream is free and what a phenomenal concept in a time where everything has a price tag, including humans and their brains. I have not seen a promotion for buying one dream to get two free, and thus it is free. Dream away, my friend, the meter is on your side still.

A dream is powerful since you can be whatever you choose with no limits. In your dreams you can be an astronaut, a king, a lion, a bird, a flower, a stream of water or even the ocean. A dream is so powerful that we, some branch of human beings, have tried tirelessly to control and limit it and will continue to do so with no notable success.

A dream is private. It lives in your mind and your soul. Only your eyes can see it. You give your dream birth, you nourish it with love and you live it privately until you decide to make it public. Even then, it is not entirely public because you still keep something for yourself.

A dream is accessible everywhere at any time with no need for special circumstances. You can dream while riding the bus, while eating, while jogging, while you're under pressure, and even while performing the call of nature. No tools are needed. No connection to the Internet is necessary. No app is required and certainly no contract. And you may be already dreaming right now. Could it be more accessible than that?

A dream requires no extra care whether you are daydreaming or night dreaming. You power it with whatever energy you have. We, humans, actually use less energy while dreaming than eating.

A dream is limitless by design. As a matter of fact, one of the purposes of dreaming is to bypass the limits we experience in our lives. Have you ever dreamed of something you already have? Or something you don't want to be or achieve? All of our dreams exist outside of our limits. It is a coping mechanism so we don't lose ourselves completely to the limits we dislike. The essence of a dream is to be out of the ordinary so why do less?

A dream is flexible by nature. It can be whatever you want it to be, any time you choose, as many times as you choose and for as long as you desire. It is as flexible as air and water, so take advantage of it and stretch it beyond the limiting beliefs that pull you back. Show your limiting beliefs what flexibility is. Just reframe your dream as you please. You'll drive your limiting beliefs crazy.

A dream is free yet it is priceless. We pay nothing to dream and we achieve our goals and desires thanks to that dream. If it were not for the ability to dream, we would have never known what we could have achieved. If it were not for a dream we would have never been able to take that first step. If it were not for a dream we would have never known that a future existed. If it were not for a dream we would have spent our entire lives around the center of our current reality. If it were not for a dream, we would be living in the caveman era. No dream equals no future. So, let me ask you about the price of dreaming. If a dream was an item in a bidding contest, and you knew that no dream equals no future, *how much would you have paid for it*?

A dream is powerful to the extent of danger. When we dream, our brains respond unconditionally regardless of the dreamer's intent and that's where it becomes dangerous. We can dream of what may be harmful and our brains will help achieve the dream. While I have always advocated dreaming away, I advocate dreaming for the good of all concerned because of the dangerous power that dreams possess.

A dream is private yet universal. The same dream could be shared among people that are miles apart in distance, circumstances and beliefs. For example, innovators or athletes or writers all have one thing in common: they dream of something yet to be created, achieved, or shared. Their dreams were private at their inception, yet the concept of raising one's spirit and serving humanity was shared.

While a dream is accessible, it is hard to come by nowadays. When was the last time you heard of a nation dreaming of achieving something and receiving the entire world's support? When was the last time you heard of an elderly person celebrating a lifelong dream he or she has achieved? When was the last time you talked to a parent bragging about his or her child's dream instead of his or her own dream? When was the last time you heard a teenager speaking about his or her dream without looking for validation or avoiding embarrassment? When was the last time you heard a child describing his or her dream without an adult doubting voice asking, "Are you sure?" What happened to "Tell me more... this sounds great" with complete sincerity? What happened to nourishing the child's imagination to thrive so humanity does not vanish? What happened to "She is only a child... let her dream"?

The few humans who are capable of dreaming, and seek no permission to do so, energize the world every day. It is thanks to Beethoven, Bach, Mozart and many others and their dreams that we hear soul-lifting music today. It is thanks to Thomas Edison, Graham Bell and Charles Babbage that we are able to perform beyond the norm. It is thanks to Shakespeare, Michelangelo, Gandhi, Gibran, and others, that the arsenal of human literature has been rejuvenated. It is thanks to Conrad Röntgen (x-ray), Alexander Fleming (penicillin), Edward Jenner (smallpox vaccine) and others that we enjoy a healthier and longer life. It is thanks to their dreams that we are energized, yet their dreams didn't break the energy bank. Any desire to have your name to join this list? If you do, start dreaming for the common good.

A dream is, by design, limitless, yet it may become limiting through our thoughts or our "conscious mind." A dream is born when you start dreaming. It grows and it continues to do so as long as you keep dreaming. The more you dream, the bigger, the more colorful, the tastier, and the more frequent and tangible it becomes. Only you have the power to kill that dream or stop nourishing it. And when you do so, you create the limits of your dreams. By consequence, the dream will limit you as well since it was limited from growing. For all these reasons, dreaming big is the way to go.

A dream is flexible yet binding. A dream binds your conscious mind to achieve its agenda. When you dream, you create an internal realization through your subconscious mind that what you see in the dream space is possible. Of course it does not start as a realization, since most of us are disbelievers and suspicious with a long history of dealing with our limiting beliefs. Instead, it starts as a fictitious idea that, when you have confidence, will become reality one day. This is what your conscious mind will tell about your dream: "It is a dream. It's nice to have one but it's better to get back to reality." For some of us, when we jump off of that limiting beliefs train and continue dreaming, we start writing a contract with our brain with all the juicy and igniting details: colors, smells, feelings, locations and timeframes. That contract will bind you, your conscious mind, to accept the new reality and get on board with the dream team to achieve the desired outcome. So think, *whatever is binding you, you created it.* I hope this helps to answer, "How big?"

N.: I believe it does. Let's get back to your dreams you had 40 years ago. What were they?

Maximus: Here we go again.

N.: Is it that uncomfortable to face what you dreamed and see if it is your new reality, Mr. Big Dreams? Or would you rather stop at the preaching station?

Maximus: I practice what I preach.

N.: Let's check. The proof is in the pudding.

Maximus: I am a dreamer, big-time dreamer. I am an achiever, big-time achiever, and I will continue to excel and thrive despite your thoughts.

N.: Easy, old-timer. I just asked for a moment of truth. Are you even comfortable going there?

Maximus: I see what you are doing, in your usual sneaky way. I beat you every time, you know, so this time is just another round. Forty years ago I decided to leave my place of birth to anywhere I could make my dreams come true. My dreams were not just for me; they were, and still are, for everyone around me. Of course, I dreamed of the big mansion with the acres of breathtaking gardens, the majestic yacht along with the red Ferrari. I dreamed of all those tangible possessions that I had no way of enjoying as a teenager. But I also dreamed of more profound matters that would give life a better taste. I dreamed of a comfortable living for my mother, siblings, extended family and friends. I dreamed of building homes for families that lived in the poverty of one room. I dreamed of building schools for unfortunate children that had to walk 10 miles each way to attend a one-room school. My God... If you saw how they were dressed and what they wore for shoes in the middle of the winter, your heart would have broken. I still have a vivid picture in my memory of the look I saw in those kids' eyes. They reminded me of a bird flock. They were nine children who did not exceed the age of 10. I remember talking to a seven-year-old boy, as another little girl held him close to protect him from this stranger, me. I asked, "How far do you still have to walk to get to class?"

He looked up at me with his beautiful, sharp, green eyes and answered with determination, "Maybe another hour." There was absolutely nothing stopping him from getting to his destiny; it was just a matter of walking the distance. The little girl shook his shoulder, encouraging him to get going before they were late for school. As they walked away he took a few steps with his squadron then he turned back toward me, without stopping and asked, "Are you the new teacher?"

I asked, "Don't you already have a teacher?"

He stopped, turned completely toward me and said, "We've been hoping to see him in class for the last couple of weeks but he has not shown up and I thought you may be the new one."

So I asked the question: "Why are you going to school then?"

He answered without hesitation, "I like to learn so that when I grow up I can teach other kids like me. I would be there every day when they came to school."

I felt waves of mixed emotions when I heard his statement. As I watched him disappear down the long road, I felt helpless. I felt incapable. I felt paralyzed. Tears filled my eyes but couldn't leave because I had a voice in my head asking me, "Is that all you are capable of—tears?"

N.: It is a touching story, I'll give you that. Which part resonates with you the most?

Maximus: If a seven-year-old boy walked 10 miles to school each day for the dream of becoming a teacher, even while uncertain if his teacher was going to show up to class, what's my excuse for not achieving my dreams?

N.: And so you decided to dream big and go for your dreams? How poetic.

Maximus: This is not new. I don't even know why I am having this conversation with you. You don't understand.

N.: Well help me understand, please. You talked in the beginning about decisions you made based on data you collected 40 years ago. Was this your data?

Maximus: That was one of many igniting sparks that led me to what came next. I knew I had big dreams compared to my circumstances. I knew I needed to make life-changing decisions if I wanted to realize my dreams. It was obvious that the source of the challenges was financial and thus, I started thinking about the possibilities of overcoming the source challenges. It was clear that my environment did not have the foundation for a financial makeover; therefore, finding the right environment was essential. I moved to what has been my new hometown for the past 40 years. When I arrived I had zilch. Sorry... I take that back, one person paid for my first grocery shopping items. I was blessed to land a job—far below minimum wage—but I was fortunate to work long hours to be able to pay rent, buy books and start my new life.

N.: And you truly believed you were going to shift your financial circumstances and achieve your big dreams with such compensation?

Maximus: I invite you to look at me, check my name, see the person I have become and be the judge.

N.: We are still on the path of answering the million-dollar question and this is only one battle in a lifelong war, so do not claim victory yet.

Maximus: Thank you for the confession. It has been a war, hasn't it? So what is that burning question Mr. Nagnag?

N.: I don't like it when you call me that.

Maximus: Are you going to deny your name? Didn't you give me the freedom of naming you?

N.: That's not our topic now, is it? Let's get the focus back on you. I see you have achieved much of what you have dreamed, if not all of your dreams. I also know you have lost things along the way as well.

Maximus: You must know by now that everything in life is a tradeoff. Some people call it investment; others call it the cost of doing business and all the rest call it sacrifice. Ultimately, we give and we take. The order doesn't matter. What matters is that giving is inevitable.

N.: We are in agreement so far. Whatever you call it, cost, sacrifice, investment or tradeoff. Has it been worth it?

Maximus: You know that "doubt" and "regret" are words that have been expelled from my vocabulary for as long as you have known me, so why are you asking this question?

N.: You are asking this question, not me. *I am only a reflection of you.* I am your mirror. I say what you make me say.

Maximus: (Whispering.) You are a pain in the brain if anything at all.

N.: I can hear that, you know. I live in your brain so I hear your thoughts.

Maximus: I know and it was intentional Mr. Nagnag. So, you want to know if it was worth it?

Nagnag: No, *you* want to know the answer to that question.

The voice, Mr. N., was a nag indeed. Maximus had given him the pet name "Nagnag," which seemed perfect at times like these.

Maximus walked toward a wall-sized double glass window, where he could see all the runways. He straightened his tie, and pulled back his jacket to put his hands in his pants pockets. He stared at the open sky as he stretched his back then he reached, with his right hand, inside the pocket of his jacket to pull out an old-fashioned watch on a chain. He stared at the watch and caressed it and as if he was trying to milk memories out of its steel material. He squeezed the watch with his big palm as if he was giving it a hug, a very warm and long one. He lifted his hand to his mouth, he kissed the watch and he asked, in a whisper "How did I do?"

He stared again at the open sky as if he was waiting for the answer. He stared at the space beyond the clouds as if transporting himself through the clouds. As he swam in his own world he heard a deep voice behind him. "Sir, your family and friends are waiting in the jet. We will take off when you are ready."

Maximus wiped a single warm tear from his cheek and, without turning to face his pilot, he asked, "Are we missing anyone?" Nearly 60 close friends and family members had been invited.

"Out of the 57 invitees, only the teacher, Sir. He left you this African bird and this piece of paper."

Maximus unfolded the piece of paper as he patted Manam, the African bird. The message read, "I promised one of my students to review with him as he recovers from illness. I know you will understand. It has been my promise that I would be there for my students always. Remember? Manam will tell me the happy details when you come back safely. I will see you soon. My forever gratitude and respect."

"Okay," Maximus said to his pilot. "Let's not keep them waiting longer. It is nice to have everyone, almost, on board." He gently grabbed Manam's cage and said, "It's good to see you buddy."

"Goooood to see you tseh...tseh....tseh... buddy."

Maximus looked back at the runway then gave one last look at the spot in the open sky as if he was still waiting for an answer to his question. He would have loved very much to hear it.

Nagnag: How attached are you to hearing the answer?

Maximus: Very much so. (His eyes filled with tears again.)

Nagnag: Is it the answer you are seeking or just the sound of his voice?

Maximus: (With a cracking voice). Both, actually. Maybe his voice more than anything else.

Nagnag: What if you do not like the answer?

Maximus: I would be content with that. He taught me how to do the work and I didn't mind fixing what needed to be fixed. He would offer advice to keep me going.

Nagnag: The advice... What about that?

Maximus: What do you mean? (He boarded the van to the jet.)

Nagnag: You have always talked about writing a book sharing the wisdom you learned from him so others can benefit, as well. How close are you to finishing it?

Maximus: This is your chance to rub it in. You know very well I have not even started it. So what are you trying to achieve from this?

Nagnag: To help you.

Maximus: You, help?

Nagnag: Give me some credit. You know I help sometimes.

Maximus: You are absolutely correct about the "sometimes" part. So what are you offering?

Nagnag: I know how much you love your grandfather. I know how much you are connected to him and how much you believe in what he thought of you. I also know how much you love the idea of spreading his wisdom and making him known to all mankind. Why would you deny yourself that reward? This is a perfect time—a vacation—to write that book.

Maximus: It is a family vacation and they deserve my attention over work.

Nagnag: Is eternalizing life lessons *work*? How true are you to yourself at this moment?

Maximus: You're right. It is more of a treat than work and I can make it happen.

Nagnag: Say that again for the love of God. I am what? I am right?

Maximus: Give me a break, will you? I have said that before.

Nagnag: Not often enough.

Maximus: Because you bounce on two ropes, my friend. Sometimes you are a nag and other times you are an igniter. You still nag, but for a good cause.

Nagnag: That's who I am. That's my job so you can be your ultimate best.

Maximus: (Smiling again.) That's a matter of perspective. So what do you suggest we do?

Nagnag: You can talk to me about what you learned. I will ask questions, as it is my nature, and go from there. How committed are you?

Maximus: Very much so.

Nagnag: What is that? You know I am a very specific kind of being. What does "very much so" mean?

Maximus: "Being" and "specific"? You mean a figment of imagination and painfully rigid?

Nagnag: I thought we were a team.

Maximus: (Smiling again.) No harm intended, Igniter. I was only teasing you.

Nagnag: I like that name. How about we keep this one and drop "Nagnag"?

Maximus: You're pushing it. And you have to earn it. So let's start an hour after takeoff so I have a chance to greet everyone, then we'll do it for about two hours every day. How does that sound?

Nagnag: Fine. What do you think will stop you or delay you from completing it?

Maximus: Maybe family activities or the desire to be lazy.

Nagnag: What will you do about that?

Maximus: Let's reserve the first two hours of the day, early morning, for this task.

Nagnag: Deal.

Maximus: Deal.

Maximus stepped onto the jet and was overwhelmed by his grandchildren's' hugs, kisses and screams—exactly what he needed. As he stepped onto the plane with Aidan and Aban in his arms, Farris hanging on his back and Karam holding onto his left leg, his daughter Leila faced him and helped him put the children in their seats. She put Aban by the window. She placed Farris next to Allen, and Karam in the seat behind Farris. She grabbed her father's neck as she stood on her toes and put her head on his chest while she whispered, "Thank you Daddy for gathering all of us. I love you."

"I love you more, my angel."

Muheeb stood up from his seat to hug his father and handed him a hardcover book. "This week's book, Dad."

"Thanks, son," he said smiling and gently touching his son's cheek. "You never miss a beat, son." As he was making his way to the back he saw Maher, his oldest, in deep thought, swimming in a pile of papers and writing away. Maximus asked with a chuckle in his voice, "Are you sure you have enough ink to capture the sea of thoughts that has taken over the plane?"

As Maher gathered his papers, he stood up to hug his dad saying, "Sorry, Father. I didn't mean disrespect. I was waiting for you when this new idea hit me and I couldn't stop it. I would love for you to be the first to read it. Will you?"

"I will be delighted, son" he said as he grabbed him from his shoulders and continued, "May your stream of inspiration never dry."

He finally made it to the back of the plane, to find his partner for life and soul mate chatting with his mother. He said with a smile on his face, "Here are my most precious powerful ladies. Sorry I'm late."

"No worries, honey. It's a vacation."

He bent over to kiss his wife, Elektra, on the cheek and squeezed tightly, yet gently, on her right arm and whispered, "Thank you for caring for Mom," then took the window seat next to her.

Then he kissed his mother's forehead and he grabbed her right hand to kiss it as she pulled it away from his face, "I have always asked you not to do that. You never listen, do you?" she said.

He laughed and followed up, "Stubborn, what can you do?" Then he asked, "I don't see Adonis and Athena. Where are they?"

Elektra answered, "My parents are back there watching cartoons with the other kids."

"Great, I am going to join them."

Flight Capt.: Sir. We are ready when you are.

Maximus: Certainly. Let's go. I'll take my seat, Captain.

Flight Capt.: Thank you, sir. Family and friends, we are taking off. Don't forget to dream a runway dream and launch it to the sky when we are airborne.

⌘ ⌘ ⌘

Dreaming is your only conduit to live your future instantly.

- *Dream big;*

- *Dream every day; and*
- *Include the rest of the practices of this book because dreaming alone is only the first step.*

Maximus, Learning from the Vault

If you don't know why, you won't know how.

Maximus: How come I can't go? Why me? I never get to do anything fun. I never get to do what I want. Why does it have to be this difficult? It's only $2.50 mom. Mom? Mom? Mom! Why you are not answering me?

Mom: Sweetheart... I would love for you to go and if I could afford it, I would have taken you out of your misery, but I don't have the money.

Maximus: But... But it's only $2.50!

Mom: I know, son. I know.

She took a deep breath through her nose, blinked her eyes and squeezed them tight, trying to hold back her tears. She grabbed her son's tiny palm to kiss it and said, "You are only six years old, and you deserve a $2.50 vacation. Maybe if I help our neighbor with some house chores I can get some of that money, or all of it." She combed his soft, thick hair with her fingers.

Maximus: Mom, I don't want you to work for another woman to make money. Last time you helped our neighbor, her son made fun of me in front of the kids at school. He said that I was poor and his mom helped you bring food home. He said I own nothing in life except the cardboards of the honorary certificates I get for my grades. He asked if I built a house with them yet so we don't have to rent.

Mom: (Not facing him and barely able to sound the words out of her mouth.) And what did you say?

Maximus: I said it was only a matter of time. *Patience and persistence always reward the resilient seeker.*

Mom: Whaaaaat? Where do you get that from?

Maximus: From Grandpa. He taught me that the other day at the river.

Grandpa: (Walking into the room.) I hear the prince of the future and the glorious life explorer mentioning my name. Was it for wisdom or praise?

Maximus turned around to face a tall, thin, confident man with striking ocean blue eyes and a smile like the dawn. Maximus screamed "Grandpaaaaa.... You're here!"

"Yes my prince. Come into my arms." Grandpa bent over to lift up Maximus, who wrapped his tiny arms around his grandfather's neck and glued his lips to his cheek for an endless kiss.

Grandpa: Haha! I still need my cheek. Make sure you leave some of it for me.

Mom: Hello, father. (She hugs her father and kisses him on the forehead.)

Grandpa: So where's this vacation, my prince?

Maximus: It is at the campground in the forest, Grandpa. All the boys in my Boy Scout squadron are going except me.

Grandpa: And you want to do the same?

Maximus: Of course.

Grandpa grabbed Maximus' hand, leading him outside the house for a man-to-man talk.

Grandpa: Why do you want to go?

Maximus: Because everybody else is going.

Grandpa: Interesting. So if everyone else decided not to go, you would not go?

Maximus: I'm not sure.

Grandpa: You said you really, really, *really* want to go and you said you wanted to go because everybody else is going. At the same, time if nobody goes you're not sure if you want to go. So, what do you really want?

Maximus : Well... Grandpa... I want to go because everybody else is going and I will have fun with them. But if they don't go, then who am I going to have fun with? Then going would not be that important right?

Grandpa: Well, son. What you want to do is up to you, not the others.

Maximus: What do you mean, Grandpa?

Grandpa: Well, if you truly want something in life it doesn't matter what the other circumstances are.

Maximus: When I go with my squadron we do a lot of good things. I learn a lot of new things such as how to tie the sailor's knots, how to do certain studies, how to learn about certain types of behavior, and how to live in the wild and survive. All that stuff is good. I love it.

Grandpa: That sounds like a lot of fun. Now we are talking. Very good, son. Continue. What else? Why do you want to go?

Maximus: I also have a chance to play with the kids and I get to wake up early with them and go jogging and play soccer and we have a fire pit at night and we roast marshmallows and we tell stories. We have this leader who is really good with stories and I love listening to him.

Grandpa: Better than my stories?

Maximus: No. You are the best. He's just different. He has other kinds of stories, Grandpa. Stories about brave boys and how they became brave leaders and how they did really phenomenal things for their families and friends.

Grandpa: That sounds very interesting. And why do you like that?

Maximus: Because it teaches me a lot of good things and models interesting behavior that I would like to follow in my life.

Grandpa: Impressive as usual. Now what happens if you don't go?

Maximus: Well I won't be able to have fun with my friends. I will not learn new things, and I will be miserable in the house.

Grandpa: If you stayed at the house, what would you do?

Maximus: I don't know, Grandpa. I'll probably spend the time reading stories, drawing and watching cartoons.

Grandpa: And how'd you like that?

Maximus: I'd like it but not as much as going to the camp with my friends.

Grandpa: Very good. So why is that not the same?

Maximus: Because it's different, Grandpa. It's just different.

Grandpa: I don't understand what is different. You can read stories at home and you can listen to stories in the camp. You can watch cartoons at home and you can play on the playground at the camp. So what is different?

Maximus: When I stay home I do all these things by myself. I can read and I can enjoy the stories, and I can enjoy cartoons but it is not the same as when I hear the story from the leader and have fun with my buddies and share stories and we discuss a lot of things.

Grandpa: I like that and I know you like discussions, too. What do you discuss?

Maximus: We discuss the stories that the leader tells us. We discuss why these people did what they did and why they were thinking that way. We also talk about why we wanted to do these things and what we dreamed of accomplishing.

After some time of walking with his grandfather, Maximus found himself at the bamboo house on the river. The same bamboo house he had been visiting with his grandfather to enjoy their endless conversations. It seemed, to Maximus, that this bamboo house on the river was the School of Life, where the visits with the most interesting and valuable man he had ever known in his life had occurred. As they entered the bamboo space they felt the cool breeze and took in the smell of the plants around them: the smell of rosemary, mint and so many other plants. As his grandfather sat down he asked him, "You know that I have always talked to you about life matters as if you were my best friend, the experienced adult in life, right?"

Maximus looked at his grandfather with his big brown eyes, he blinked a couple of times and he said, "Of course, Grandpa. I love our conversations and I wish they would never end."

His grandfather grabbed Maximus' face between both hands to give him a kiss on his forehead and said, "You are the wisdom of the future, my son. If I could pour into you everything I know about life and everything humanity has witnessed I would do so. I hope I can do some of that before I depart."

Maximus looked at his grandfather with his big eyes and asked, "Are you going somewhere, too?"

His grandfather chuckled then answered, "No, my prince. That's something you will learn about some other time. Let's get back to the topic of the day: your vacation." Grandpa pointed at something in the south corner of the bamboo room where they were sitting and said, with his deep voice, "Look, Maximus. What do you see there?"

Maximus got closer to the corner of the room and said, "A long line of black ants."

Grandpa: What are they doing?

Maximus: They look like they're moving stuff from one place to another.

Grandpa: Great. Look deeper, what else do you see?

Maximus: I see them moving as if the day is ending. They are going very, very fast and in both directions and they're not stopping.

Grandpa: Why do you think that is?

Maximus: I don't know.

Grandpa: My prince, of course you do know. You just need to think a little deeper.

Maximus: I think they are trying to get something done before something else happens.

Grandpa: Something like what?

Maximus: I don't know, Grandpa.

Grandpa: Think a little harder. Try to focus a little more.

Maximus: Grandpa, why do you want me to think all the time? You always ask me to think harder and deeper. How do I do that?

Grandpa: You are absolutely correct, son. I know I push you to think harder and deeper but never told you exactly how. Yet magically you do a great job every time.

Maximus: But I don't know if I'm doing it right this time.

Grandpa: Talk to me about it.

Maximus: When you tell me to think harder I think more and more and I don't find myself seeing anything but then I start looking into what you asked me to think about in different ways. For example: what if this happened or what if that happened or what if nothing happens. Do you know what I mean?

Grandpa: Beautiful, my son. That's exactly it. That's why I said you will be the wise one of the future. You are naturally wise and I would love for you to care for humanity as you grow up.

Maximus: Humanity? What is that, Grandpa?

Grandpa: Mankind, my prince. That's everyone you encounter in life. That's your fellow human beings whom you see every day, and the ones you don't see.

Maximus: Even girls?

Grandpa: Today's girls are tomorrow's ladies, my prince, and they will need your wisdom, your respect, and your care more than you think. Do you see anything different about the line of ants?

Maximus: No, Grandpa. They are still going as fast and as determined as I saw them a couple of minutes ago.

Grandpa: Why do you think that is? Have you determined what they're trying to get done and why?

Maximus: It looks like they found a good piece of bread that they're taking as tiny pieces and they are transporting it to somewhere else, a place that I cannot see.

Grandpa: Let's imagine for now that they're just taking it to their home. What do you think about that?

Maximus: That seems reasonable. They are probably going to eat it later.

Grandpa: So what is that thing, that they are concerned about, that would stop them from doing what they need to do?

Maximus: Maybe they are afraid that another animal would come and take the piece of bread. They may also want to finish before the night comes?

Grandpa: Very good possibilities. What other possibilities may exist?

Maximus: Hmm, I'm not sure, Grandpa.

Grandpa: Are you giving up?

Maximus: You taught me never to give up in life.

Grandpa: That's correct, my prince. You are correct never to give up because when you do what happens?

Maximus: You told me the other day *when you give up you lose the taste of life.* I don't know what that means but I'm sure that I will know one day like you told me.

Grandpa: Since you're not giving up, what other things or other obstacles are these ants worried about?

Maximus: They seem to be in a hurry to get this piece of bread home. How about a hint? Don't give me the answer.

Grandpa: Let me give you a little hint. Do you remember the story of the ant and the grasshopper?

Maximus: Oh yeah, of course I do. I read that some time ago. I still remember the happy grasshopper was having the time of his life while the ant was trying to get everything... Oh... I got it, Grandpa. They are trying to get the piece of bread to their home before the summer is over, right?

Grandpa: That's exactly it, my son. You see how capable you are when you put your mind into it?

Maximus: But you helped me, Grandpa. You gave me a hint.

Grandpa: That may be true but we all need that little nudge to move forward and that's okay. That's what just happened. So you're saying the ants are going so fast because the summer may be over soon and winter is coming so they want to have their food ready for the wintertime, right?

Maximus: But summer is long. Why are they rushing as if it was ending today?

Grandpa: That's true son, summer is long but look at the pieces they are taking from the big piece of bread. How long do you think it will take them to transfer that to their home?

Maximus: It will take them a very, very, very long time. You're right, Grandpa, they want to make sure they have the job done before it's too late. May be they can finish before the summer is over and they can dance with the grasshopper.

Grandpa: Now let me show you something.

Grandpa walked to the line of ants and put a little stick right in the middle of the line and said, "Let's see what happens, Maximus." As they both watched the line, Maximus said, "Oh look, Grandpa! The ants got scared for a few seconds, and they didn't know what to do, but then they figured that if they go over the stick they can just keep doing what they were doing before."

Grandpa smiled. "Now let's see what happens if we put a shorter stick just a little further from the first one. Let's try it and make sure we are not harming any of them." He grabbed a little stick and put it a few inches away from the first one and told Maximus, "Watch what happens."

Maximus: They didn't do the same thing this time. They just went around the stick.

Grandpa: Why do you think that is?

Maximus: Maybe because the first one was very long so if they did to go around it they would waste too much time. The second one was higher, but shorter, and may be they figured out that they can go around it so they don't have to go up and down too much.

Grandpa: That is exactly it, my son. Now the big question is, did they change their mind at any point?

Maximus: No, Grandpa. They just kept going.

Grandpa: Why do think that is?

Maximus: I don't know, Grandpa. Maybe because summer will end soon for them and they will not be able to take the entire piece of bread home?

Grandpa: That is the apparent reason. Let's think deeper. If you were one of these ants, what would you be thinking right now?

Maximus: I know you're going to tell me to think harder Grandpa, so I'm going to think.

Grandpa smiled and raised his eyebrows, nodded his head in agreement and stayed quiet. A few minutes passed by, then Maximus spoke.

Maximus: If I was one of them I would be thinking "I have all of this big piece of bread that we need to take home and I cannot take the whole piece of it at once. I can only take tiny pieces and it is going to take me forever to do it. I need to work very, very hard so I can get the job done before the winter comes."

Grandpa: Very good. Now what happens if you're not able to transport all of it to your home before the winter comes?

Maximus: That will not be good, Grandpa, because I will not have enough to eat for the winter and the winter is very long and cold.

Grandpa: So how important is it that you need to finish the job on time?

Maximus: Very important, Grandpa. Extremely important, Grandpa. If I don't do it I may die of hunger during the winter season.

Grandpa: That's it, my prince. Do you know what we call that?

Maximus: I can take a guess. I would say we call it "why the ants do the job they do."

Grandpa: That's pretty much it. In more fancy words we call it, "the real reason." You see, my prince, there is a real reason behind everything we do. There is a reason for everything that happens in life.

Maximus looked up at his grandfather without any clue of what was said. He did not have the words to ask the right question. Grandpa was perceptive enough to see that on Maximus' face, so he resumed by saying, "I know it may be difficult to understand this concept at this age, my prince, and I also know how smart and wise you are and it will make sense to you once the time comes." Maximus felt a little intimidated so he tried to show that he was old enough by raising his chest and putting his hands on his waist.

Maximus: Of course I can understand, Grandpa, just tell me more.

Grandpa: Let's take a walk by the water.

As they walked side by side next to the water, Maximus could not bear the silence anymore and he grabbed his grandfather's hand and asked, "Grandpa, I know that you want me to think and you are giving me time to think, right?"

Grandpa: Correct, my son, what have you come up with?

Maximus: Well I have a question first. You said the "real reason." Is that different from the reason?

Grandpa: In most cases it is. We do things in life and we believe, many times, that we know the reason for doing them. However, it takes much more understanding, and very deep digging into our feelings and souls, to land on the *real reason* behind doing what we're doing. Quite often we find, after a lot of digging, that the real reason is different from what we always thought the reason was.

Those phrases passed by Maximus like any other breeze that he felt during that walk. They didn't really make sense. He couldn't think too much about what his grandfather said but he knew that if he couldn't understand it at that this point, he just needed to keep it in mind because it would be understood later, "once the time was right," like his grandfather always said.

Grandpa: At first when I asked you why you think this line of ants was doing what they were doing you came up with quite a few reasons. Then when I asked you to imagine that you were one of them, you came up with different reasons.

Maximus: Yes, Grandpa.

Grandpa: There was a difference between what you initially thought and what you found out later after more thinking and questioning, right?

Maximus: Yes.

They walked side by side silently for a few minutes. Grandpa was walking by the water and holding Maximus' hand. After a few minutes, Maximus stopped and slipped his hand from his grandfather's big palm, grabbed a stone and threw it in the water. He walked closer to the water line and watched the ripples expanding one after another. He stayed still for about a minute, looking at the center of the water ripples, and then he turned to his grandfather and said, "I always like what happens after I throw a rock in the water."

Grandpa: You mean the ripples?

Maximus: I like how they go from one tiny circle to many large ones. And you taught me that the bigger the stone, the bigger the ripple in the water. But the part that I don't understand is why they are circular all the time. Most of the stones I throw in the water are not circular, but the ripples are. That tells me that what I think is the reason for the circular waves, the stone, is not the *real reason*. This is difficult. But it is good.

Grandpa: Why is that?

Maximus: It helps me learn more, understand better, and I can teach my friends.

Grandpa: You just listed three reasons. Which one of them is the real reason? (Smiling)

Maximus: Honestly? I think it's the last one.

Grandpa: And why do you think the last one is the real reason?

Maximus: Because it makes me feel so good to learn something new and to share it with somebody else.

Grandpa: How does it make you feel?

Maximus: I feel strong. I feel I know more, and I feel I can do more.

Grandpa: And how do you like that feeling?

Maximus: I like it very much, Grandpa. I think it is what I will do when I grow up. Be a teacher like Mr. Simon. I like him. He knows a lot of stuff and he teaches us a lot of new things every day. Everybody loves him and everybody respects him.

Grandpa: How about a spicy sandwich, my prince?

Maximus: That sounds really good, Grandpa. You can read how my stomach thinks.

Back on the plane...

"Grandpa, it's sandwich time. Grandma is asking if you wanted your spicy sandwich or a sweet sandwich." Maximus barely open his eyes, turned his head to look at Karam, and he stared at her eyes for a few moments until she said again in a patient tone, "So, sweet or spicy? Which one, Grandpa? Come on wake up."

Maximus smiled and answered, "Spicy sandwich, my princess."

"Do you feel okay?" his wife asked. "You missed the takeoff. You never miss takeoff. That's your favorite part of the flight. Is everything all right?"

"I was just spending some quality time with Grandpa."

"How was it my love?"

"It was one of the fundamentals he taught me many, many moons ago. I think he may be reminding me of what is important and why we do what we do. He was wise, grounded, cheerful and comforting as usual. I was blessed to have him for the short period of time that I did."

Elektra brushed his silky gray hair with her nicely groomed fingers, then grabbed his right cheek between her fingers and said with a big smile, "And we are blessed to have you."

At a loss for words, he grabbed her hand that touched his face, kissed her palm and put it against his heart. "And it is a blessing to have you make my favorite sandwich. Sweetheart, would you please call Maher to see me? Thank you, honey."

Maher: Dad, did you want to see me?

Maximus: I still see your hands filled with your paperwork instead of your sandwich. You're not even with your kids?

Maher: I really need to finish this before we land.

Maximus: Come sit with me for a few minutes, will you? Aban, would you please bring your dad's sandwich to him? He would really love to have it from your hands.

Aban: Of course, Grandpa. (To Maher.) Here you go Dad, I hope you enjoy it.

Maher: Dad, I really need to finish this. I can eat the sandwich later.

Maximus: Son, why are you doing this much work?

Maher: Because it is very important.

Maximus: Son, help me understand what it means to you.

Maher: Dad, corporate is waiting for this paperwork from me and I am expected to deliver it within 72 hours. It is important, Dad.

Maximus: Your dedication and sense of responsibility are truly appreciated and valued, my son. What you just told me is what is important to corporate. What I asked you was how is it important to you?

Maher: It is important to me because it is my responsibility to fulfill my promise and get it done by the time I'm expected to deliver.

Maximus: Which one depends on it the most: your happiness or your wellbeing?

Maher took a long deep breath, held it inside for a while as if he were starving of oxygen, sat back and exhaled.

Maher: Certainly not my life. Certainly not my wellbeing. It is somehow related to my happiness because when I get it done I will feel happy.

Maximus: Understandable. Why did corporate give you a task right before you left on your vacation, knowing that you asked for this time off six months ago?

Maher: Truth be told, Dad, I have had this task for the last two months and I have not been able to finish it. I procrastinated and put it off every time it came in front of me.

Maximus: So how important is it again?

Maher: I know, Dad. Clearly it is not important enough to me.

Maximus: Why is that, son? You have always been determined and clear on what you wanted to do. What has changed?

Maher: Dad, you know that play that I have been writing for the last 10 years?

Maximus: Yes, "Love in the Typhoon Era," what about it?

Maher: It has been haunting me for the last six months. I wake up in the middle of the night thinking about it.

Maximus: So you wake up in the middle of the night to finish writing it?

Maher: Not quite. I stay still, staring at the ceiling until I fall asleep again. I am torn between two aspects. Two opposite aspects. A big part of me is really in love with writing and would love to finish this play and get on to the next one. The other part tells me I have enough time to do it whenever I choose.

Maximus: I'm going to ask the question that you have not been able to ask yourself out loud. How prepared are you to hear it?

Maher took a deep breath, looked outside the window and stared at the clouds underneath the plane for a good while, as if he was looking for something. Then he said, "I think it is time. Ask away, please."

Maximus said, "On second thought, I am quite confident you know the question. How do you feel about sharing it with me?"

He took another deep breath, with his head between his two hands, rubbing his face intensely. He turned around to face his dad and smiled. "I feel like it is the old days, Father. I feel like I'm 10 again, when you used to ask me these kinds of questions. You actually never stopped asking me these heartfelt questions. I just learned over time how to navigate through them. It always comforted me, knowing that you are here and you will always keep asking me these questions.

Maximus: Stop talking. You have not shared the question yet, or are you navigating away again?

Maher: No. I don't want to navigate away anymore. I'm just collecting my courage to face you.

Maximus: You are my son, and you know better. How true is it that by asking the question you are facing me?

Maher: You are correct again, Father. I will be facing myself.

Maximus: That's my boy. And as always, you know that you share only when you are absolutely comfortable.

Maher: Of course, Dad, and here it comes.

Maher looked outside the window again and he whispered, "If I truly believed that I can write my play anytime I choose, while I know that I have a strong desire to do that, then why have I not done so? What is stopping me?"

Maximus: Sorry, son, I could not hear that very well.

Maher: What is stopping me from finishing my play if I truly desire to finish it? What am I concerned about? What am I afraid of? Why do I keep interrogating the writing process every time I sit down to write? Why has it been 10 years since I wrote the first line of the play? Why have I been sitting back watching everybody else writing their plays, achieving success, while I am simply telling myself that I can finish whenever I choose but I still don't finish? What do they have that I don't? You know, Father, many times I think that I don't have what it takes to finish the play. I think that all the other writers are able to finish because they have the skills to do it, and if I had what they have, I would've probably finished mine and I would've probably written nine more.

Maximus: Son, do you think you don't have what they have?

Maher: Help me with that. I don't see what you mean.

Maximus: You know that through your high school years you were among the best writers in your class. The awards you collected and the praise you received exceeded all expectations. You were even invited to write this play at the age of 19. You had the luxury of no time limit that I have never heard of. What does that tell you?

Maher: Thank you, Father, for lifting my spirits, it truly feels good. While I doubt my writing ability every once in a while I am confident of what I can do and what kind of writer I am. Thank you for reminding me.

Maximus: I think that takes care of the skills, right?

Maher: Yes.

Maximus: That's the part that they have and you also have. Now, what do you think they have that you don't have?

Maher: The desire.

Maximus: I believe you have the desire to write. If it were not for the desire you would not wake up in the middle of the night.

Maher: What is it then? I am exhausted and feel lost.

Maximus: What was your favorite activity when you were growing up? Think back to when you were a child, when you had nothing to worry about except what you wanted to do.

Maher: I used to immerse myself in books and in my essays. I wrote, almost constantly. I saw myself in the world that I wanted to live in. I made my reality. I captured the essence of the people around me. I created new people with their life aspects, their emotions, their goals, their individual and collective journeys and even their perspectives about life and death. Writing was my existence. And I have not felt that way for a very long time. I wrote because I knew why I wrote. I wrote because it gave me existence, gave me a life, and gave me a reason to live.

Maximus: Now that was very beautiful, my son. That's what your grandfather called the *real reason*. It is what we call nowadays the burning desire or the "burning why." When the reason for doing anything is important enough that it is a matter of existence, a matter of life or death, a matter of identity, a matter of being, that's when you know why you do what you do. When the "burning why" keeps you awake at night, takes you to a world different and distant from your daily world, you know that you have the real reason. When the "burning why" jolts you every time, you back off and you think of giving up on your dreams, you know that you have the real reason behind your desire to achieve your goal. Any dreams you have for as long as you live on this Earth will never go any further until you know the "burning why".

Maher: I remember the words you taught me when I was in high school. I even wrote them on a piece of paper that I always kept in my desk drawer: "To go from dreaming to any other stage of the achieving journey, you need to find out the 'burning why'. The success train will never leave the dream station until the burning why conductor is leading the head of the train." I even had a sketch that you did yourself of a young man standing at one side of a river on a wood bridge that had only one piece. On that piece, where he was standing, there was the word "Dream." In his hand, he had another piece, which he was about to place next to the one that he was standing on to build the bridge. That piece had the words "burning why" written on it. He carried other wooden pieces on his back that he was going to place on the bridge structure each time he added a step.

Maximus: Thank you for reminding me, I forgot all about that. I am glad I left it with you so it is not lost forever. So tell me, why now?

Maher: What do you mean?

Maximus: You have been working on this play for ten years. You have not written for a very long time. Why now?

Maher: Because I am tired of being somebody I'm not. *I am exhausted fulfilling a role that was not meant for me.* I have learned from childhood to live for what I believe I was sent to this Earth to do. Yet, I lost my path and I miss it, and it is time to go back to it.

Maximus: What makes you think that going back to writing is what you truly are looking for?

Maher: I am certain. Nothing I do in life makes me feel more fulfilled than writing. I still write every once in a while. Every time I take a moment to write, I feel reborn. I feel exactly what I felt when I was growing up. When I write, I know I have a message for humanity that will shape people's lives and bring them to think of more possibilities that will lift their spirit beyond their wildest dreams. I just need to write.

Maximus: How likely is it that the "burning why" inside of you right now will be put out anytime soon?

Maher: It has been that way for the last 10 years, but it won't be like that anymore. You know exactly why I write. It is my existence. I gave up on my existence for the last 10 years and I am not willing to do that for the rest of my life.

Maximus: You are an inspiration, my son. I hope nothing more for you than to stay hungry to be who you are meant to be. This is a transformation, my warrior. When are you going to begin?

Maher: Right away. I can't wait to hold the pen.

Maximus: What about your 72 hours deal?

Maher: Right. How about I make a deal with you? I know I can finish the paperwork that I have by the time we land. I will get that out of the way and send it to the office. I will go then with a clear mind to focus on writing. Focus on being me again.

Maximus: How thrilled are you about this approach?

Maher: As much as I am thrilled you are my father, my teacher, my mentor, and my centering spirit.

Maximus: I wouldn't go that far, son. I am satisfied and grateful to be your father. However when you get as old as I am, Mother Nature will call you more often than it used to.

Maher: I don't follow. Am I missing something?

Maximus: You are right now, son. You won't be though if you don't stop talking and let me go to the men's room, immediately.

Maher: Sorry, Father. I am still in my dreamland. Yes please, go ahead.

As Maximus stood up, he turned around and placed his knee on his seat, grabbed his son's face with both his hands, squeezed his cheeks like he used to do to him when he was little, and gave him a kiss on his forehead. He looked very closely into his eyes and said: "Welcome back, my prince. You never lost anything, you just took a break for soul-searching and came back stronger, more determined, and destined for your life purpose." Maximus got up again and brushed his son's hair as he tried very hard to keep his emotions in check and went on his way to the call of nature.

Maher: Hey, Dad, you just gave me the idea for my next play.

Maximus: We'll never disagree about royalty fees. (Smiling)

As Maximus made his way through the aisles to go to the men's room, he brushed all the heads of his grandchildren on the way as if he was passing by a wheat field and caressing its crops. He closed the door behind him, and as soon as he did so he heard his best buddy saying, "You did fine work there. Not bad."

Maximus chuckled and said, "I wouldn't be able to sleep without your confirmation, Nagnag."

Nagnag: What was the thing with your grandfather that you
talked to your wife about?

Maximus: May I have some privacy?

⌘ ⌘ ⌘

If you have not achieved it yet, check the principles of *the burning why*:

- *Why this?*
- *Why now?*
- *How persistent is my desire (how burning is the "why")?*
- *How soon can I start?*
- *What may stop me and what am I going to do about it?*

Omar, The Man Who Can

"Whether you think you can or think you can't, you're right."
-Henry Ford-

Nagnag: You are back to your seat, and you are comfortable. So what happened with Grandpa back then?

Maximus: Well, do you remember the story about when I was six years old and I wanted to go to the camp with the Boy Scouts and my mother didn't have $2.50?

Nagnag: I think so. You bring it up every once in a while but you never told me the entire story.

Maximus: Of course you don't know about it because I was a kid then and had no room in my life for limiting beliefs. You had no control over me then. The story ended with a couple of sentences between my grandpa and me as we were going home to get that spicy sandwich. After the long conversation we had at the river about the *real reason*, he asked me on the way home if I knew the real reason behind my desire to go camping with the Boy Scouts. I remember thinking for a few moments and then I told grandpa that I wanted to prove to my Boy Scouts squadron that I was not poor and that my mother could afford $2.50 and I was not any less than any of them. *That* was my burning why.

Nagnag: I am still curious as to how that is related to what you shared with your son.

Maximus: That will be in the book that we talked about earlier at the terminal, so you will have to find a way to read it.

Nagnag: My dear friend, you forgot about the power of our partnership. I will actually have a sneak peek of the book before the world. I will read it through your thoughts even before they become words on paper.

Maximus: You're correct. Wait, wait—did you hear that? What my granddaughter said?

Nagnag: No I didn't hear her. What was it?

Maximus: Karam, my princess, you have always been the best at telling stories. My best storyteller can't tell a story to her mommy? How come?

Karam: Because I can't Grandpa. I just can't.

Maximus: I never heard you saying you can't before today. Come to Grandpa, princess.

His daughter said, to her daughter, "See how you got your Grandpa worried about you?" Then she turned to Maximus. "She's been like that for the last couple of days, Father. I don't know what she learned recently but she has been repeating it more frequently."

Maximus: I know what my princess wants. Come here, honey. Come sit with Grandpa. I miss you and I miss your stories.

Karam: But I have no story for you, Grandpa.

Maximus: Then it is time for me to tell you a story.

As soon as he finished his sentence all the children raced to their grandpa's seat, chanting all together, "Story time... Story time... My Grandpa will give me a dime."

Maximus said, "This time you give me a dime because I am telling the story."

"But I don't have a dime, Grandpa," said Aban as he stood next to his grandfather's seat, lifting his shoulders and raising his palms to the sky to show how empty they were, and blinking his eyes as if he was asking for sympathy.

"Kids, I have your dimes here if you let me listen to the story with you," said Muheeb.

"My Uncle will give me a dime," said Aban, as he raised his arms up and shook his hips left and right.

Nagnag: What a deal you got there, buddy. I envy you.

Maximus: Stay out of it, will you? It's family time. We'll touch base later.

Then Maximus said, in a louder voice, "Yes, my son is taking care of his own and his nephews while his father is doing all the work. You see that, Elektra?"

"I am actually joining them as well. Your story for a dime, a deal no one can beat," said Elektra.

Karam: Remember everyone this story is for me. Right, Grandpa?

Maximus: Absolutely, my princess. So whom do you want to keep
out of the story time?

As she looked around and found all eyes looking at her, begging in silence and waiting for her decision, she looked down, took a deep breath and raised her tiny shoulders, then said, "No one, Grandpa. I love all of them. They can listen, too."

"That's my wonderful princess," said Maximus. "I know you have a heart as big as the universe and love that fills the hearts of all humans."

"Thank you, Grandpa, that's what my mommy says, too. So what's the story about?"

As everyone gathered around Maximus, he grabbed Karam and placed her on his lap, fixed her dress, and gently put his palm on her tiny chest and said, "Your Highness, Princess Karam, today's story is about Lily and Carmen, the monarch butterflies."

Maximus: Lily, a monarch butterfly, laid about 100 butterfly eggs
in our neighborhood park. Lily was always caring and
paid extra attention to her new babies. She was blessed
with a long life and a loving heart to make sure that her
babies would hatch out of the eggs from the moment
she laid them inside of some plant leaves. Lily always
had healthy babies. With her extra care, all of her
babies hatched out of their shells and became beautiful
monarch butterflies.

This time, Lily had a different feeling about the wellbeing of her babies. She knew that the weather had changed and she thought that her babies needed more care, so she decided to follow their development even more closely than she had done before. Before laying her eggs at the park, Lily made sure to lay them all in the same area so it would be easier for her to check on them and keep an eye on them, like your parents do for you.

For the first period of their growth, the baby monarch eggs are as big as sesame seeds, and as time passes those tiny eggs grow little by little to become shells. When the time is right, the babies start eating the shell from inside to nourish themselves, gain strength, and make an opening so they can come out. As usual, all the babies made it out of the shell almost on time and they stayed close to the shell, eating more of it so they could have more nutrition and grow even bigger.

However, weeks passed and one of the shells did not open. Lily became concerned about her baby. She landed on the almond tree leaf and watched the non-cracked shell for a moment. She walked around it just to see if there was any sign of life. She didn't see anything. She got closer and knocked on the shell with her tiny hand saying, "Rise and shine, baby, it is beautiful out here, are you on your way out?" Lily heard nothing and she became more worried. She used both of her hands this time and pushed the shell forward to see if she could hear anything and she repeated, "Rise and shine, baby, it is beautiful out here, are you on your way out?" Still she did not hear anything. Lily became concerned that she had lost her baby and she could do nothing about it, so she was about to fly away.

But then she reminded herself that she had never lost a baby before. She thought to ask herself how she could give up on this baby. She sat there for a long time thinking, wondering what to do next. She was sure that her baby was still there and could make it out. She wished that she could go inside and make an easier route for her baby butterfly to enjoy life. But she didn't know how. All that Lily learned in her life was how to come out of the shell, but she had never learned how to go back inside. After a little bit of thinking she knew that only her baby could crack the shell to come out. She was determined to think and think and think even harder to find a solution and not lose her baby. But she also knew deep in her heart that she needed to think differently to make her wish come true. While she didn't know what exactly to do next, she was confident that her baby was still alive inside and able to make it out. She knocked on the shell another time and she said, "Carmen, Carmen, honey, I am here. I am your mommy and I know you are coming out. I know you're full of life because you are my baby. It is so beautiful here. It is spring. Everything is flowering and the colors are endless. The world is just waiting for you to enjoy it. I know you can hear me. If you hear me, move in any direction."

As she stayed there for a minute waiting for her baby to give her a sign of life, Lily prayed for her creator to give

Carmen strength so that she could enjoy life. To Lily's surprise and pleasure, the egg wiggled, just a tiny bit. Lily jumped up and down, thanked God for the sign of life, keeping her tears inside and getting closer to the shell saying, "Honey, Carmen, baby I know you can hear me and I know you are inside. You can't wait to come see Mommy. Come on, honey, come out."

"I can't," said Carmen from inside the shell. Lily didn't know what that meant. All that she knew about her species was what they could do. They did not have the word "can't" in their minds. It was the first time she had heard it and she didn't know what it meant. Because butterflies just make it happen. They're full of life. They exist so they can make life better, more colorful and pollinate the plants.

Karam: What is "pollinate," Grandpa?

Maximus: Very good questions, Karam. This means to help plants grow more and get fruit.

"Ooooooh," all children said at once in astonishment.

"So what did Lily do?" asked Karam.

Maximus: Lily asked Carmen: "What do you mean, you can't?"

"I don't know how," Carmen said.

"Oh my sweet baby, that's very easy. Just start eating anything you see."

"But... what if I can't?"

"Honey, you are a butterfly, you can do anything. That's the only word we know, sweetheart. We don't know the other words. We don't know 'can't.' We make the world a better place. Did you know that you have 99 brothers and sisters waiting for you? Did you know that you have a whole park full of roses and flowers and plants waiting for you? Did you know that there's a whole world waiting for you to make it more colorful?"

"99 brothers and sisters? Do they look like me?"

"Yes, they look like you and they're waiting for you."

"But I can't see them."

"Because they are outside, honey, and you are inside. Once you come out of the shell you will see them and play with them."

"I don't think I can. Can you help me out of here?"

"Carmen, honey, only you can help you come out of there. Think of your brothers and sisters. I can imagine you playing with them, flying in circles, making waves in the air, and going from one flower to another, eating their sugars and helping them grow even more."

Carmen stayed still for a few minutes without any sound or sign. Lily became more worried so she said, "Carmen, sweetie, you can do anything you believe you can do. Put your tiny arms on your left side of your body, and touch your heart. What does your heart tell you?"

Carmen stayed quiet for a few minutes then she said, "Mommy, I want to play with my brothers and sisters. I want to see you and hug you. I think I can do this. Where should I start?"

"That's my brave daughter. I will knock on the shell and you will follow me. You and I, together, will find the best place to start eating." As Carmen and Lily exchanged knocks on the shell, after a minute they found the best place to start the work, then Lily said, "Honey, you must be hungry by now."

"I am starving, Mommy."

"Very well, honey. Start eating here." As Carmen devoured the spot where she started eating it didn't take but a couple of minutes for the egg to crack and Carmen's head to poke through. Lily danced around her baby, flying in happy movement, celebrating and singing, "Here's my baby Carmen." As Carmen pulled her tiny body out of the shell, Lily landed back on the almond tree leaf, showering her last baby with kisses and hugs and celebrating her success. "I knew you could do it! I knew you were a believer. I knew you could do it."

"I am happy to be here, Mommy. What do we do next?"

"Eat everything around you and let your belief lead you."

"I feel very full, Mommy. I don't know if I can do that."

"Carmen. Honey, you are here in front of me and you see the world as it is waiting for you only because you believed that you could do it. Nothing will stop you from playing with your siblings, and enjoying the world except your belief. You are here now because you believed you could do it and you will be there in a few weeks because you believe you can be there."

"And if I don't believe, what happens?"

"Then you won't be there. The world will be missing one butterfly that was going to make this place much better than it is right now. Your siblings will miss you and you will miss a beautiful life. So what are you going to do?" Carmen was quiet again. There was no sound or indication of movement as she turned around to her shell and started eating.

As Lily flew around her, she heard Carman saying. *"I believe... I believe... I believe... I believe I will grow and glow ... I believe I will shine like a glorious pine ... I believe I will dance and celebrate every chance ... I believe I will leave a colorful trace in every place... I believe, I believe."*

Maximus looked at all of their smiling faces, as they waited for the rest of the story.

Carmen ate her shell, ate the leaf that her shell was sitting on and she moved on to the rest of the leaves of that branch on the almond tree. It was just a day later that she left her first skin to grow to a longer caterpillar. She continued to grow every couple of days until the moment it was time for her to hang down for the last shedding process. She hung down for 10 days with no sign of life. Lily watched Carmen all along during the process. She knew that her warrior baby would not give up on herself. She knew that the belief she had in herself, her ability, and in the life she wanted to live, exceeded her fear. She knew Carmen was full of life. Lily wanted to see the first few moments of her baby becoming a fully-grown butterfly. She wanted to see the colors of her baby's wings as they developed. On the 11th day, as Lily was flying close to her baby, she saw the last skin opening slightly as Carmen pushed herself out, little by little. As Carmen made her way out of her last skin, her wings were tiny, however by the grace of her creator they grew to fully colored wings in less than a half hour. Carmen flapped her wings and took off her last skin, leaving it hanging on the almond tree branch. She would not go back to it again. As she danced around with her mother, and made waves in the air, her siblings flew in a big circular motion celebrating the cycle of life. Carmen chanted again, *"I believe... I believe... I believe... I believe I will grow and glow... I believe I will shine like a glorious pine... I believe I will dance and celebrate every chance... I believe I will leave a colorful trace in every place... I believe, I believe."*

Flight Capt.: Family and friends, we start our descent to Morpheus Island. We should hit the runway in 20 minutes. The weather outside is phenomenal, so descent and landing will be pleasant. Please take advantage of the slow descent and enjoy the view.

None who had gathered to listen to the story moved an inch, as if there had been no announcement made. Karam asked, "Mommy, did it take me too long to eat my shell and come out?"

Leila laughed quite pleasantly and said, "No, honey, you did not waste any time and you joined us right away."

"Okay kids, let's take our seats," said Muheeb.

"Thank you, Grandpa. I loved the story," said Karam.

"I am glad sweetheart. I am glad."

As Karam made it to her seat next to her mother and tried to buckle her seatbelt for descent, she heard her mother talking to herself, "I can't seem to find my seatbelt. I can't find it."

"I don't know what 'can't' means, Mommy, here it is. I know you can do it."

Leila had no prepared answer for Karam's transformation, but she found herself hugging her and thinking, "I wonder if the story was more for me than it was for my daughter."

"That was perfect timing, wasn't it? I know you had nothing in mind for little Karam, But I know you are more than capable of coming up with something," said Nagnag.

As the plane descended, Maximus touched the watch inside his jacket and, without taking it out, he caressed it and whispered, "I know you're here, Grandpa. I hope I learned well from you. I hope I am living up to your expectations. I hope I am nourishing your legacy from the same river of wisdom you used to nourish me. I know I am not done. I am only checking in with you and I miss you."

"Family and friends, welcome to your vacation. We will see you outside in a little bit," said the captain.

As everybody stood up to get their luggage, the plane door opened and a minibus stopped to collect the family and head to the resort.

"Muheeb, bring Manam with you, will you please?" said Maximus.

"Where do I find him, Dad?"

"He's an African bird son, just call his name and he'll call you back," answered Maximus with a big smile on his face.

"Right... that makes sense" said Muheeb as he smiled back at his dad. Maximus' oldest son enjoyed a bit of ribbing with his dad, though—as the eldest—he often spoke to him quite formally.

As Maximus approached the minibus door he found his longtime friend Omar opening his arms with a large smile on his face. As they embraced, Omar said with his British accent and deep voice, "God bless you, my good friend, and keep your heart warm for the warmth you give all of us."

"I am blessed, my good friend, and my heart is warmed by the warmth of yours," said Maximus, as he grabbed him by the shoulders and looked deep into his eyes and they shook hands in a certain sequence as if it was a secret handshake.

"What did Amir chose for his major?" Maximus asked Omar.

"It was a long and beautiful process that led him to that life-changing decision. I will tell you about the details once we get the family on the way to the resort. Amir sends his love and promised to come see you while you are here."

"I would love that. I would love to see the rest of the family."

"Of course that's if they don't make it your way first," said Omar as he giggled and grabbed Maximus by the right arm, leading him to the bus door. As Elektra and the kids greeted Omar, Karam stood back, watching how the family greeted him and then she approached him and looked up at him. She grabbed his khaki pants, pulling on them to attract his attention to her.

"Excuse me, sir, it is my first time meeting you. What is your name, please?"

Omar kneeled, brushed her hair with his left hand as he extended his right arm to shake her hand and introduced himself, "I am Uncle Omar. I am an old friend of the family. I know you are Karam, the daughter of Leila. I also know that you like butterflies—monarch butterflies," he said as he smiled.

Karam: Oh... You are Uncle Omar who sends me the monarch butterfly postcards for my birthdays. I have been waiting to meet you. Thank you very much for all the postcards you sent me. I have all of them hanging on the walls of my bedroom. Every time you send me a postcard, I memorize the names you give them. Do you remember their names?

Omar: I don't think I can, sweetie. I am too old to remember.

Karam: You don't think you can? I don't know what that means. Have you heard the story of Carmen, the monarch butterfly, from Grandpa?

Omar: No, sweetheart I have not. I guess I missed that one and I will have to ask him about it later.

Karam: I think it's a good idea, Uncle Omar. You will learn a lot from it, like I did.

Karam spoke with such conviction and confidence that made Omar laugh and nod his head in agreement; then turned to Leila and said, "Your dad is always on the go and always trying to make a difference, isn't he?"

Leila replied, "You know my dad, that's what he does and that's what he lives for. I needed to hear that story myself, Uncle Omar. It's great to see you. I missed you." She finished her sentence as she wrapped her arms around him and gave him a loving hug.

"It is great to see you, too, my sweetie. You have always been my favorite, and I appreciate you not sharing that with your siblings. I miss our conversations. How do you feel about catching up later, after you settle in?"

"That sounds wonderful," Leila said.

"Welcome, family. It is always a pleasure to have you here. All on board. This is your captain. Buckle up for joy."

In one voice, Muheeb, Maher, Leila, Elektra, Maximus and his mother responded in a cheerful tone, like they had done in the old days, "Aye, aye, Captain," followed by the children on the bus repeating the same sentence: "Aye, aye, Captain!"

Ring ring... Ring ring...

Cindy: Hello, Leila?

Leila: Oh my God... Cindy... I miss your voice... How are you?

Cindy: I am good... How are you? Am I going to see you today?

Leila: I don't know what the family plan is... But I guess this is a vacation, right? Are you here at the resort?

Cindy: No, I'm home but I can ask my dad to bring you with him when he comes back for a bite.

Leila: Yes, I would love that—especially if Uncle Omar takes me in his Jeep... I miss those days.

Cindy: Okay, hold on... My dad is waiting for you outside to bring you here. I am so excited!

Leila:(To Elektra.) Mom, I would like to go with Uncle Omar to visit Cindy for a couple of hours. Would it be okay if I left Karam with you?

Elektra: Of course, honey, she's having fun with the rest of the boys and girls. Give them my best and tell them I will come to see them soon.

Leila: Thank you, Mom.

Leila kissed her mom and headed toward Omar, who was waiting in his wild ride Jeep. "Karam is very smart and looks very much like you. She actually reminds me of you when you were her age. She has your confidence, strong personality, and quick reactions," said Omar as he was weaving between the trees, taking Leila to see Cindy.

Leila: I'm not sure if that is still the case, Uncle Omar.

Omar: How come?

Leila: Just life, things are not the same, and we learn to adapt, right?

Omar stayed quiet, as he was certain she would continue building on what she said. He was surprised to hear these words from her, because he knew how confident and certain she was, yet he wanted to know more without asking.

Leila: How do you deal with that, Uncle?

Omar: With what, sweetheart?

Leila: How do you deal with... uncertainty. The feeling of inability. The lack of drive to do what you have always dreamed of doing?

Omar reflected for a couple of minutes then he asked, "Where is this coming from?"

Leila: I don't know, Uncle. It seems that life has its own plan and we're supposed to respect it and adapt to it. Dreams are great but they don't necessarily work in alignment with what life has for us.

Omar: That's almost exactly what I said to your father 25 years ago, when we met on this island.

He took a right turn and stopped the Jeep. They stopped at a cliff with a view of the ocean, the sky and a little piece of land that didn't have much visible about it except one tall building. He turned the car off and said, "Twenty-five years ago, I worked in that hotel that you see down there, as a busboy. The only restaurant the hotel had at the time was on the first floor. One night, I went to clean my fourth table right after the waitress said that the customer was done. I headed there with my cleaning supplies, dragging my feet, thinking it was just another table to clean. I saw this young man—your father—counting his dimes and quarters and I immediately thought, "Here we go again. Another bum who is not going to pay the bill and he's going to keep me company tonight washing dishes." As I made it to the table, I slammed my bucket on it and I said in a rude tone, "So have you done this before?"

"Counting dimes and quarters? Yeah, I'm pretty experienced at it by now."

"No, smarty-pants, cleaning tables and washing dishes for your meals?"

"Oh, I already paid my bill."

"So why are you counting quarters?"

"I didn't have enough to tip the waitress well, and did not have the heart to leave without tipping the busboy. I thought if the busboy found whatever I was able to leave for him, he would either appreciate it or curse me, but he would still have something."

"I'm sorry. That was very rude and judgmental on my part. I appreciate your thoughtfulness. It's been a long day, and I am tired. Forgive me please. You don't have to leave me any tip."

"Understood. You have a tough job. I see a lot of potential in your face. What made you settle for this job?"

"We all have obligations in our lives and this is my way of fulfilling my responsibilities."

"That's very honorable of you. An honorable man like you, with the potential you carry with you, would certainly have dreams. Forgive my intrusion but I find it difficult to believe that your dream was this."

"Dreams are great but they don't necessarily work in alignment with what life has for us. So we just have to adapt."

"May I share a personal belief with you?"

"Be my guest."

"What I hear you saying is that you are settling for what you think you have from life. How is that different from adapting?"

"Yep, that's exactly what I need to brighten my night. Advice from a broke psychologist. Is that what you do? Do you go around and offer free advice that you can't afford yourself? Look at you counting quarters."

"You are partly correct. I am broke and I have been offering advice for free, relatively. But it is not true that I cannot afford it."

"Listen man, I have a lot of work to do and you sound like you got nothing to do. I'll come back to clean the table when you're done counting your quarters. Better yet, don't bother. You need those quarters for yourself."

I left to clean the other dozen tables to come back later not finding him there. Instead I found three well-organized rounds of dimes and two quarters sitting on a piece of paper. The paper read: "You only achieve when you believe. I believe in you as much as your wife and child believe in you. How much do you believe in you?"

I grabbed the piece of paper and the coins with my right hand while I had held another plate in my left hand and I ran outside of the restaurant looking for this man who believed he knew me. I did not see him in the hotel lobby. I ran outside the hotel to see him standing by the light post, next to his suitcase, as if he was waiting for somebody or something. I ran to him without stopping and as soon as I got close to him I threw the money and the paper at his face. "Who do you think you are to talk about my wife and my son the way you do? Where do you know my wife from? I swear by my son's life if you don't get out of my sight right now I will make you disappear forever!"

He answered calmly, "You came running after me and you are asking me to disappear? I don't know your wife and I didn't know you had a son. You did not come after me just because I was talking about your wife and your son. You came after me because I was the only one in a long time who held the mirror in front of you."

"Who are you?"

"I am Maximus. I empower strong-willed dreamers striving for success to achieve their destiny and I can help you create realities to live your destiny."

I remember laughing very hard and sarcastically, and telling him how pathetic he was. I told him that he was not even capable of giving me a full tip in bills; that he was collecting coins just to pay my tip and that he could not help himself, let alone help me.

I remember saying, "How can you help me achieve my dreams and success if you are not successful yourself? Unless your dream is to pay your bills with coins and your destiny is to live out of your suitcase."

"Let me ask you a question, Omar," he said. I remember getting livid for a few seconds wondering how in the world he knew my name, but it was written on my apron. Then your dad said, "You go to the bakery every day to get a loaf of bread. You never wonder if the baker has bread himself. You just know that he can make bread for you. You take it and you go home happily and you go back the next day. Think of me as the baker. It's not important if I have bread or not. It is not important if I am successful or not. What is important is that I can deliver the foundations of the principles of success the same way your baker delivers bread to you. I can show you how you can design realities and live your destiny. Now let's get to the bottom of this. If you found the secret formula that would help you live your dreams, how likely is it that you would reject it?"

"What... What are you talking about? Man, you are out of your mind. You are full of it and you don't know what you're talking about!"

I remember your dad standing there, crossing his arms with his right foot stepping forward and a big daring smile on his face while I was spinning in my place saying the same words again and again. A few minutes later I took a deep breath, looked at the ground for a few seconds and looked at him. I asked the question that he was waiting for me to ask. "So you're saying that you can help me achieve my dreams?"

"No, I'm not saying so. I know so. With a little caveat."

"I knew you were a phony! So what's the catch, to meet at the North Shore when the pigs fly at dawn?"

"The catch is you. You will get out of this as much as you will put into it. You will embrace triumph, you will taste success, and you will fly with the eagles as long as you are willing and ready to do so."

I will always remember how cracked my voice was and how hard it was trying to hide my emotions when I answered your dad, ""I... I'm desperate. I have been willing and ready. Somewhere in there I gave up. I hope I'm not too late."

"You are never too late. You are perfectly where you're supposed to be to launch. So where do you want to land?"

I remember taking a long, deep breath. I remember keeping my eyes focused on the ground because I did not want him to see my tears. I remember staying quiet for a long time, because every time I attempted to speak my emotions took over, so I held back. I remember how patient he was and how concerned I was that his patience would run out. And it didn't. He stood there until I collected myself and felt comfortable enough to say, "I have always dreamed of having my own tourist bus company with five employees and 12 buses."

"Impressive. Quite specific. You are already ahead of yourself. I'm curious, why five employees?"

"We have five hotels on the island, so I envision dedicating one bus per hotel to offer full service. The other five buses are backup because I believe in 100% service. The other two buses are for VIPs."

"Nicely laid out. Good plan. What has been stopping you?"

"I have no money to buy the buses or pay the drivers. It's not rocket science."

"Okay, let's just have a few seconds of the dream. Let's dream that you have the money right now. Close your eyes, if you need to, and see that you have the money that you need to do everything you want. What is your next step?"

"What do you mean? I... I... don't know what you mean. How can I close my eyes and imagine that I have all the money I need when I know I don't?"

"You just try. How much money do you think you need to buy 12 buses and pay the salary of your employees?"

"I don't know... I have never owned buses, and have never paid employees before."

"Why not? Just try to live the dream. Imagine you are going now with all the money you need to buy the buses and have all the employees you need to hire and that you are going to pay their salaries ahead a of time. It is all a dream, go ahead, and dream away."

"I can't."

"What do you mean, you can't?"

"I don't know how."

"If you don't know how in your dreams what makes you sure that you would know how in reality? Just try."

"I can't. I don't know how. I just... I am done with this nonsense."

As soon as I finished my sentence, I remember a humongous man standing in a front of me, pointing down at me with his strong middle and index fingers glued together, pounding on my heart and telling me in the most certain and convincing tone I have ever heard in my life, "You mean you don't believe you can achieve. You mean you don't know how to believe that you are actually successful. You mean you don't have the power, even in your dreams, to believe you can live your destiny. If you have no belief, you have no power. Here's the deal, Omar, you have to believe to achieve. Most of us know how to dream and some of us know why we dream those specific dreams, but very few of us believe that we can achieve those dreams. If you were riding on the train of your success journey, belief is the fuel of that train. Right now you have no fuel, that's why your train has not moved. And until you decide that you believe in possibilities—in yourself and in the change you wanted to be, in your ability to reinvent yourself and your ability to redefine all aspects of life—your success train will remain at the stuck station."

That was the last thing I heard from him that night as he stepped away, grabbed his suitcase and vanished into the darkness.

I could not sleep that night. His words echoed in my head and, every once in a while, I would go back to what he told me about the mirror, and the more I thought about it the more convinced I became. He was correct. He was the first person to hold the mirror to my face. I got to thinking about everything he told me and I had mixed emotions. I was so angry with this stranger who thought he had the right to tell me what he told me. At the same time, I was questioning my ability to do what he asked me to do. On one hand, I wished that I could talk to him again to understand more of his principles; on the other hand, I wanted to see him again to give him a piece of my mind. I wanted to see him again, and I didn't know how. It was clear that he lived out of his suitcase so he was not a guest at the hotel, and I had no idea where he was staying or when he was leaving. The next day, as I was heading to the restaurant to start my shift, I saw this skinny, tall man with a suitcase in his left hand and a beige hat on his head talking to the doorman. I thought it was your dad, but I was not sure. As I got closer to the door I knew it was him, but I didn't know what to say. He turned around and he said ,"Hello, Omar, I came by to—"

"To finish the delivery of the lesson, or maybe to give the same lesson to the doorman?! You just live in your La La land. You have no clue."

"No, I came to apologize. I had no right to jump on you the way I did, although I may have an explanation. I do have a clue and that's why I do what I do."

"I'm just curious, what would be your explanation for doing what you did?"

"Because I care. It kills me to see dreams die in the human heart while nothing is stopping them from thriving except the human mind."

"And why do you care?"

"Because I have been there, and because I am committed to not go there again. And I want to empower the world one person at a time: to bridge the gap between their disbelief and what they can do and what they can achieve."

"I still don't get it. Are you God's messenger to humanity?"

"I believe we all are. Every one of us is a messenger with a specific message. Few of us act on the value of that message. Some of us come to this life and leave their message buried inside of them. And some of us don't even realize they have a message. If we all realized that we have a message, and worked to make it serve humanity, the world would be a continuously and exponentially thriving place."

"What do you get out of it?"

"I get to design realities and live my destiny with all of its bells and whistles."

"And here I am, I always thought I was too much of a dreamer, only to meet a mega version of myself. Now I appreciate everything you said, but it is difficult to believe that you do this for free while you live out of your suitcase. Am I going to pay you a royalty of some sort if I achieve the success that I have always dreamed of?"

"That's a very good question. How much would you pay to achieve your dreams?"

"If I was certain that by following your principles I would achieve success, then I would pay anything."

"I am going to ask you a favor. I would like for you to repeat your last statement without the word 'if.' Would you please?"

"Now, I know you are a dreamer and I appreciate that, but forgive me here for saying this is quite silly. What a silly request!"

"What do you have to lose? Just give it a try."

"Okay... okay... I am certain that by following your principles I will achieve success and I will pay anything."

"I'd like for you to say it three times, and say it as if you mean it, without the paying part, please."

"I am certain that by following your principles I will achieve success... I am certain that by following your principles I will achieve success... I am certain that by following your principles I will achieve success."

"How does it feel?"

"It feels right. It actually feels good," I said as I smiled and I truly felt that Maximus would empower me to bridge the gap between where I was and my destiny. Maximus helped me believe. Since that day I completely removed the words "I can't," "I don't know," "not sure" and similar types of expressions that had disempowered me for my entire life up until that point.

I remember him asking, "So... How committed are you to achieving your dreams? To *creating reality and living your destiny*?"

"I am committed all the way, but I have two questions that have been bugging me and I would love to know their answers before we go forward."

"Sure, what are they?"

"How do you know my wife and my son?"

"I don't. It was an educated guess. You had a wedding band on your finger, you had an aura of a very dreamy powerful man yet you carried energy that said all over you that you were in the wrong place. You also had a very worried look on your face that, while I could've understood as dissatisfaction about your lifestyle, I had a feeling that it was more than that. So I thought you might have a child you were worried about. But I had no clue that your child was a boy. What is his name?"

"He has not made it here yet, so he does not have a name yet but we know he's a boy and I know his abilities," I said that with "a proud smile," as your dad described it back then.

"I am certain he will be strong, and optimistic, like his dad is. Okay, what is your next question?"

"Why do you say create realities and live your destiny instead of create *your reality* and live your destiny?"

"I love your attention to details already. You will make a phenomenal business owner. Only *you* know your destiny and only you can truly live your destiny. However, when you create your reality, you impact the realities of the people around you and end up designing their reality with or without a choice. In return you create theirs with or without a choice. Therefore when you create your own reality you actually create a reality as a whole for the purpose of living your own destiny. Satisfied?"

"Well, I know that you're smart enough to know that I have nothing to pay you now."

"You can think of it as an act of paying it forward. It would be great if you could focus on our collaborative relationship more and less on the logistics. Payment will take place. I have no worries about it and I hope you don't."

Omar: And the rest is history, sweetheart. That was the lesson that I learned from your father—the lesson that changed my life and drew the launch line for my success journey. I am, and will always be, grateful to the Lord for him. And I am and will always be an ambassador of his message.

Leila: Wow! No one told me this story before. When I asked my father how he knew you, he said that you were one of his teachers in life, that he learned so much from you. He never told me details but he said one thing every time I asked him. He said that he learned from you that *the human belief never disappears or expires, it just gets hidden and buried underneath the layers and layers of circumstances to which we all believe we are destined to adapt.* Then the moment we decide to believe again, all it takes is just to dust it off and we are already up and running. The sky is the limit.

Omar: I know I don't have the charismatic teachings that your father has and I just told you my story instead of asking what you wanted to talk about. But somehow I believe that the essence of my story applies to everyone and that you could learn something from it.

Leila: I actually learned exactly what I needed to learn. My father was always keen on dreaming big and the "burning why." With me he was never keen on the belief part, probably because he never saw in me the lack of belief. But over time I lost that power and you just brought it back, Uncle Omar. Thank you.

Omar: I'm happy there was something useful in what I shared with you. Oh look... We are late for lunch and I'm sure Cindy will give us another lesson when we get there.

Leila: No worries, Uncle. I'll vouch for you.

Leila's laughter and her spirit were lifted many levels. The story that Omar had shared with her gave her the answer she was looking for. What made her day even more joyful was the time she spent with Cindy. While they enjoyed their lengthy replays of childhood memories, they connected the dots to the present. It was another confirmation for Leila that what, as a child, she had believed her life would be had come true. When she made it back to her room she ran to her journal, as she used to do when she was a teenager. She wrote:

Today was a phenomenal day. I learned from my daughter and I learned from my Uncle Omar. My daughter gave me the chance to listen and to learn with her a life lesson from Dad. I think my father was sharing that lesson with me as well. The same life lesson I heard a few hours later from Uncle Omar, who had a real-life experience with my dad applying the belief principle. I pledge, as of today, that I will never forget the belief principle, its derivatives, and what they stand for. As my commitment to live by this principle, I am writing down its cornerstones so they shall be my reminder whenever I need to believe in all the possibilities. Believing in possibilities raises my awareness and my conviction that I have more ways of achieving my dreams. It guarantees to me that if one way doesn't work, there is an abundance of other ways that will work. As I believe in the abundance of possibilities I will believe more in myself and in my ability, too. Believing in oneself will defeat self-doubt. I realize that, since my teenage years, I have left out a very important lesson. I left out the importance of actually living the dream in my mind and in my heart. While the dream lives in the mind, the belief lives in the heart. I know when I believe I have the sense of owning the world. I have the sense of having unlimited power. I have the sense of redefining all definitions. As I believe I am living my dream I redefine time, obligations, wants and desires, ability and power, and myself. I redefine myself, my environment, and the world around me. I am empowered to reinvent my circumstances and my reality. I know that I create reality and live my destiny as long as I believe. Believe, for it is the only way to achieve.

As she closed her journal she heard Karam from her room asking, "Mommy, are you coming to tuck me in?"

"Of course, honey, I am coming." Leila laid down next to her daughter and asked, "How do you like the vacation so far?"

Karam: I like it very much, Mommy. I love playing with my cousins, swimming, and spending time with Grandpa.

Leila: Grandpa loves that, too. Did you have fun with him today?

Karam: Yes, I loved the Carmen story. I will never say "I can't" anymore.

Leila: So what are you going to do when there is something that you may not be able to do?

Karam: I hear Daddy a lot of times, after you ask him to do something, say something that I think I like.

Leila: What do you mean?

Karam: You know, when you ask him to do certain things, he says, "Let me see what I can do." He whispers right afterwards, "I am not sure what I am going to do but I'll figure something out." I think I like that. From now on instead of saying "I can't," I will say "Let me see what I can do." What do you think, Mommy?

Leila: I think that's the best answer I have ever heard. You are my inspiration, my love. You truly are. Get some rest, you have a long day ahead of you tomorrow.

Karam: Really? What are we going to do? Tell me, tell me! Exciting stuff?

Leila: Yes, honey. Exciting stuff but you need to get your sleep because you need all of your energy tomorrow. Night night, baby.

Karam: Night night, Mommy.

⌘ ⌘ ⌘

To reinvent yourself you've got to:

- *Believe all is possible.*
- *Believe in yourself.*
- *Be the change.*
- *Live the part.*
- *Redefine time and space.*

The Tough Lesson

A mirror a day keeps the blame away.

The day started with a beautiful dawn, clear sky, light breeze and birds singing and celebrating a new beginning. It was the day Muheeb had planned for the family. He was the first to wake up, to check the weather. He thought, "This is a perfect day to be with nature, connect with our souls in peace and harmony, and to give the kids a chance to learn from the birds, the bees and the little details we miss through our daily lives in the city."

He woke up Aidan and Aban. He asked Aidan to walk to the other rooms and wake up all the kids and his grandpa. It didn't take long before everybody gathered in Maximus' room with their backpacks, excited and ready for the journey.

"It is going to be a day like no other. It is going to be the journey of your life. It is going to be the highlight of your learning experience," said Muheeb with endless enthusiasm and excitement.

Elektra said to Maximus, "Honey, I am going to stay with Mom. I'd rather spend some time with her here, then we will visit Omar's house to spend time with his wife and his daughter. I haven't seen them for a long time. Have fun with the boys. It will be more fun for you guys without worrying about us. What do you say?"

"But I would love for you to be with me, honey," said Maximus.

"I know, but I also know that you like hiking and you know how much I like it," she said as she giggled and her face turned red.

"I understand and I would like for you to be comfortable."

"Thank you, honey. I will see you guys when you get back. Have fun and be safe."

"Let's get out of here so we can start," said Muheeb loudly, his voice filled with excitement.

Muheeb: Dad, are you ready?

Maximus: I was born ready, son. How about you?

Muheeb: My father always taught me that I was born ready.

Maximus: Anything I can help you with, son?

Muheeb: I got it, Dad, no worries at all. Okay everyone... we will have short rest periods along the way before we get to our first stop by dusk. We will spend the night there. Next we will go around the island to come back here. This is your last chance to change your mind; otherwise you are in for a treat.

The kids looked at each other and resumed their jumping with excitement. Everybody was prepared with their backpacks on their backs, properly dressed and armed with the right attitude for the journey. The sun showed its top glorious half, lighting the faces of the travelers. The breeze continued to assure everyone that the journey would be pleasant and the birds were singing along with the boys. Muheeb walked a few feet away from the group, signaling with his hand for everyone to get going. They started walking toward the forest, leaving the resort behind. Muheeb was a phenomenal Boy Scout leader. He spent quite a few years learning through Boy Scout events. He learned that exploring facilitates soul searching. He learned that connecting with others is a guaranteed way to build self-confidence. As he walked with his troop, family members started humming one of his all-time favorite Boy Scout songs. As he hummed his song, the boys behind him followed his lead. To his surprise, his son Aidan learned that song from him some time ago and had taught it to his cousins. The humming turned into loud whispering and the loud whispering turned into full-fledged singing.

Walk and walk in the road racing your company...

Walk and walk laughing cynically at any obstacle in your journey...

Drop the dusty city far, far behind your back...

Sing, sing the song of hope so the universe will sing it back.

As Muheeb led his company, his father walked behind everyone, making sure that he was the last. He had learned from his own Boy Scout days that this formation created a complete force moving together in unity. He felt fortunate to see one of his favorite songs passed from his Boy Scout leaders to him, to his son, to his grandchildren. About three hours later, the troop stopped for a quick break. "Uncle Muheeb," asked Farris, "How long are we going to walk?"

"Are you tired already?"

"No, not really. I just want to make sure that I use my energy wisely."

Muheeb answered his nephew, "That is wise by itself. You are absolutely correct and we all shall understand and learn from what you just said. Yes we have quite a bit of distance to walk."

"How far are we going?"

Muheeb answered, "We will reach our destination after the sun goes to the other side of the sky. However, we will stop every once in a while for a quick break, so we can eat and drink something before we walk again. How does that sound?"

"That sounds great, Uncle. Thank you."

"Okay, everyone. Who can tell me why some of these trees grow up straight and some of the others grow up crooked?"

As the kids looked at each other trying to figure out the answer Aidan was quiet. After a few minutes, Muheeb asked, "So what is it, Aidan? What is the answer?"

"They're striving for one of their basic nutrients: sunlight. If you look at the crooked trees you will find them planted next to bigger trees. As they grow, they move around trying to reach the sunlight. And because they move around in different directions, that's what makes them look crooked."

"Wow, you are very smart, Aidan," said Karam.

"I'm just older and I know a little more; and now you know as much as I do," said Aidan.

"Time to get back on the road," said Muheeb. "Ready everyone?"

The boys stood up to resume their circular motion as usual, singing and dancing. "We are all in... and no one is out, we are all in... and no one is out," they sang. A few stops later, as fatigue started showing on the children's marching, Maximus asked Muheeb, "How are we doing on time? Do you want us to speed up?"

"I believe we should be all right."

Maximus noticed some hesitancy in his son's voice so he said in encouragement, "Aye, aye, Captain, it should be what you say. We'll follow your lead and we trust your ability."

"Right... We should be okay."

It was about an hour before dusk when Muheeb set his backpack on the ground, laid his map next to it, kneeled and started drawing lines on his map and scratching his head. Maximus saw how he was concerned and worried but he also understood that it was his time to reflect and find out the right next step to be taken. Maximus took advantage of the moment to ask for a break for everyone and gathered the kids around him so they could have a family game.

Aidan didn't want to leave his dad scratching his head by himself, so he joined him. After a few minutes of looking at his dad playing with stones on the map, he asked, "What is it, Dad?"

Muheeb: I'm trying to figure out how we ended up here.

Aidan: Isn't this where we are supposed to be by this part of the trip?

Muheeb: It doesn't look like it, son. But I don't know how we got
here."

Aidan: We got here based on how we walked so far.

Muheeb: Aidan, I really need more than wisdom at this point.
Will you look with me on the map and see where we
missed our path?

Aidan: Of course, Dad, I'll be happy to do that. I just remember
that we came to a couple of forks and I remember you
standing in the middle of the road taking one of them. I
believe that's what got us here.

Muheeb: I know, son. I know. Let's figure out which one so we can
find a way back to get on the right path.

Aidan's character was the most similar, among all the family
members, to his grandfather's. He was quiet, calm and confident.
He spoke only when it was necessary, and spent most of his time
and energy listening and reflecting on what he received. He spent
a lot of time with his grandfather and Maximus loved spending
time with him. He was the first grandchild of Maximus, who was
very excited to share with Aidan everything he knew, the same
way his own grandfather had shared with him. Aidan always asked
to go with Maximus to seminars and workshops, spent time with
him at home, and even spent time with him at his office whenever
he was preparing a book. He learned tremendous wisdom from
his grandfather at a very early age. He was even built like his
grandfather. He was tall for his age, slim, with olive skin, thick
long dark hair, beautiful, sharp and big hazel eyes, long eyelashes,
full eyebrows and very confident and pleasant presence. All of his

physical and soft attributes helped him become really popular in school without him making any effort. Whenever he was asked what he wanted to be when he grew up, he always said, "I would like to do what my grandfather does." For a seven-year-old boy, it was quite a treat to see how confident of his life purpose he was. He knew how to speak about his life purpose, how to address everyone's needs around him, and how to be there whenever he was needed.

Aidan knew deep inside that his father had made a couple of turns on the way to their destination that were not the right ones. Yet he did not want to make that apparent. He just wanted to help his father see what had happened.

Aidan: You see, Dad, you have this marquee on the map. That's where we started from the resort, right?

Muheeb: Yes, son, I see that.

Aidan: I don't see any lines on the map that show the initial routes that we were supposed to take, but I see the stones that you placed on the map. Those stones are the road forks where we stopped a couple of times and we took the turns that got us here?

Muheeb: Yes, son. That's right.

Aidan: I'm sorry, Dad. I don't see our destination on the map.

Muheeb: What do you mean? We're going to this park right here in this area.

Aidan: That's a pretty big area. Where exactly in that area are we supposed to be?

"Let me see here, one second." Muheeb took a few minutes struggling with the map, turning it right and left, upside down and right side up, and then put it back on the ground with the stones on it. "You are correct son. We are where we are because of the routes we took."

Aidan: And that's perfectly all right, Dad. As long as we know where we are and know where we want to be.

Muheeb: Oh, my son. You spend so much time with your grandfather, and I'm grateful for that. I remember when your grandfather taught me that lesson when I was about your age. I remember him saying, "Always remember you are now here based on the decisions that you made before now. Today is always the result of the past."

Aidan: Yes, I remember that perfectly and it is one of my favorite sayings that I have in my room on my desk.

Muheeb: Okay, what can we do now?

Aidan: We do what we're supposed to, Dad. We know where we need to go. We need to trace the routes, estimate the time and take action.

Muheeb: Yes, son, that sounds really positive and easy but I don't think we have enough time to go back on the road to get where we intended to be. If you look closely at the map, you will see that there is no direct way from here to where we need to be. We need to go back a good distance to get on the right path to the park.

Aidan:(Shuffling the map.) You're right, Dad. What do we do now?

Muheeb: There is a nice area on the map, not too far from here; I believe it would be good for us to spend the night there. It is quite a change in the plan but it is part of the journey. Right?

Aidan: That's what makes the journey pleasant.

Muheeb: Okay, let's figure out the right way to bring the news to the family and have a clear plan for what we do next. Shall we?

Aidan: I am with you all the way, Dad. But you can tell everyone.

Muheeb: Of course. It is my responsibility and I would never put it on your shoulders. I'm the captain, right?

Aidan: Aye, aye, Captain.

They walked together to where the family was gathered. "All right everyone, I have good news and bad news. Which would you rather hear first?"

Maximus spoke softly saying, "You pick, son. We will deal with both."

"The good news is that we are going to walk less than we expected by this time to reach our destination," he said, and stayed quiet for a few moments hoping that he would hear cheers from everyone so he could continue with the bad news. Contrary to his expectations, everyone was actually waiting for the bad news at this point. "Our destination for tonight will be different than what was planned initially. We will be camping tonight at a nearby park. We will have fun for the night as we planned and early in the morning we will resume our journey to the park that we were supposed to visit and spend the night. Come on everyone," Muheeb insisted, "This is part of the beauty of the journey, right?"

When no one answered, he tried another level of encouragement. "Outstanding, let's get going so we can make it to the park on time and we can start our evening activities of fun and enjoyment. We'll have a campfire, we have marshmallows, and we can share stories..."

Everyone dragged along in displeasure toward the new destination. Muheeb could see the disappointment on the children's faces and he felt a weight on his shoulders. An hour later, they arrived at the campground and it was time to set up the tent.

Setting up the tent was Aidan's favorite task in camping so he led the effort and he made sure that everyone had enough enthusiasm to get it done in a short period of time. He kept promising everyone the marvelous sunset waiting for them once they got the tent ready. Aidan hoped to bring everyone's spirits up so they could enjoy the rest of the trip. When Aidan finished his job, he made sure that he delivered the baton to his father: "Aye, aye, Captain. The tent is set. All the belongings are inside. Beds are set. Everyone is enthusiastic and can't wait to have fun. We're ready for you, Daddy."

It actually worked and lifted Muheeb's spirits, and he announced, "If we walk to the shores now, we will catch the sunset right before it starts. It will be the best sunset you will ever see and you will ever remember. Who is with me?"

Everyone screamed, "We are all in!" That gave the boys permission to do their victory dance. Their singing brought everyone back to life and lifted their spirits. They walked with enthusiasm and joy. All the couples walked close to each other, and all the grandchildren walked with Maximus as if they understood that this moment meant something different to them than it did to their parents.

It was a majestic moment when the sun touched the water. While it was not the first time that the family had watched and enjoyed a sunset, it was the first time for all of them to see that particular sunset—at that specific place on the globe, at that unique moment in time.

Maximus moved his head in a funny motion that only he understood. He drew a check mark as if he was confirming to the universe that this task was done. He held his grandchildren closer to him. As they all watched the sun going down bathed in a glorious shine from the waters of the North Shore, he spoke to his grandchildren in his usual soft, deep, tone. "My princes and princesses, take a mind snapshot of what you have right now, for this moment and others, to enlighten your future."

"What is a 'mind snapshot,' Grandpa?" asked Karam.

Aidan jumped to answer the question. "Think of your eyes as a camera that will capture everything it sees at this moment and take a picture. Think of your ears as a recording device that captures all the sounds around you at this moment. Embrace the feelings that are swimming inside of you, engrave them on your heart so that you can come back to them whenever you need."

Maximus was proud to hear that description from Aidan. But he also knew that he needed to explain to the rest of the grandchildren, so he resumed, "Sweetie, try to remember everything you see, hear, and feel about this moment."

"Why do we need to do that, Grandpa?"

"Because every moment we live, sweetheart, becomes the past as soon as it passes. The only way to live that same exact moment again is in your memory."

"You mean like what Mommy felt when she gave birth to me because I am unique and she can't make another one like me?"

"That is perfectly correct, my princess. You are unique and no one else in the world will be like you. And Mommy will always remember the moment she gave birth to you in her memory but she cannot make it again in life, because that was a special moment for you and her."

"I understand, Grandpa, I understand. Okay, let me focus so I can put this moment in my memory."

Maximus was pleased with the discussion he had with Karam; he grabbed her closer, kissed her head then brushed her shiny golden hair. As it started getting darker, everyone stood up to head back to the campground. It was time to relax, have some food, and enjoy the night's entertainment that Muheeb had planned.

"Please grab any dried tree branch you find on your way," Muheeb said. "We will use that for the campfire tonight as we gather to listen to one of Grandpa's stories." As soon as they made it back to the campground, they piled up the sticks in the middle.

Aidan: Wow, Dad. That was a brilliant idea. Look how much we have.

Muheeb: A heavy load is as light as a feather to the group. You never heard Grandpa saying that?

Aidan: No, Dad. What does that mean?

Muheeb: It means what would be a heavy load for one person would feel as light as a feather when carried by a team. Union is force and union makes everything heavy seem light.

Aidan: Wow... I like that.

Muheeb: Sometimes I get the drift of your grandpa's wisdom.

Muheeb laughed and pointed to the pile, signaling to Aidan to add his branches next to the pile and carry on. Muheeb prepared the fire pit so that the fire would last through the evening. The others had their own tasks to do before dinner was served. About an hour later, everyone was sitting around the fire with sandwiches and ready for Grandpa. Maximus sat on the sandy ground, leaning against a tree behind him while he faced everyone and asked, "What are you in the mood for tonight?"

Karam spoke up, "Another butterfly story, Grandpa."

"Let's hear something else," said the boys.

"If you do not like Karam's suggestion, then you should present your own," said Maximus.

"Dad, how about that story with Grandpa when you were in high school? I have not heard that since I was in high school myself," said Muheeb.

Maximus nodded in agreement as he looked at the ground, thinking that it would be a good opportunity for his son and his grandchildren to hear that story. Maximus began...

It was many, many moons ago. I was in high school and I was passionate about sports, the outdoors, and human behavior. While I was very active in these areas my grades were not that encouraging in the rest of my classes. It was the last quarter of the school year when I realized that I needed a miracle to pass to the next level. You see, high school back then was different from high school today. Every student had to have a passing grade for the entire year to be able to progress to the next grade. There was no summer school. It was just the school year. If a student didn't pass, that year was to be repeated. It was another year that everyone else in the class would pass, and I would miss being with all my friends. It was another year of not progressing in life, because at that age, school was the measure of tracking progress in life.

It was the month of April and I had about two and half months to make something happen so I could secure a passing grade. I was listening to the radio when I heard, 'Where's the prince of the future and the glorious life explorer? I have not seen him for a while. Will the birds show me his location?'

I remember feeling uncomfortable, and rather ashamed. I felt ashamed because I was listening to the radio while I knew that it would take a miracle for me to pass to the next grade. And I also knew that if my grandfather was aware of it, he would not be pleased with me. And probably would stop calling me the Prince of the Future and the glorious life explorer. It was a big name for me that I lived up to until that moment and it was very difficult for me to let my grandfather down. At the same time, I didn't know exactly what to do. So I answered, "I am here, Grandpa," while I jumped out of my place and turned the radio off. I attempted to grab one of my books but I was not successful because Grandpa made it to the room before I did.

Grandpa: How's my prince doing?

Maximus: I am all right, Grandpa. I am okay.

Grandpa: Just okay? What seems to be occupying your mind?

Maximus: Nothing much, Grandpa.

Grandpa: That's a concern too, my son. If nothing is on your mind then you're not thinking. Life is full of matters that would make you think, and keep your mind occupied. I know you don't live an empty life so that tells me you have something on your mind that you're not telling me. How true is that?

Maximus: That is true, Grandpa. I just don't have enough courage to tell you.

Grandpa: Courage is not what you're missing, my prince, as you have always had enough of it. You are worried and I would like to make it easy for you if I can, but I will not be able to do that if I don't know what it is.

Maximus: You're right, Grandpa. It's about school. They say that I am not in a good position to pass to the next grade and I would need a miracle.

Grandpa: You sound displeased and in disagreement with what they tell you.

Maximus: Of course, Grandpa, I have been doing everything to get good grades and pass. I have been doing everything to learn. I've done all my work and everything that was required. And now they tell me I cannot pass unless I have a miracle?! They are just being unfair. My teachers are not even taking into consideration the effort that I put into my homework. They don't care if a student passes or not. They make the classes difficult and the exams even more difficult and they expect us to learn and be successful. I'd rather spend my time on the things I like. I love playing sports, I love writing and drawing, and I love the outdoors. Sometimes I think they're just wasting my time or they're just doing it on purpose. I know that I have done everything possible to be successful. I know if they were just to consider all the effort I invested in the last six months they would find that I am more than qualified to pass to the next grade.

Grandpa: That must be frustrating, son. Where's your mother? I don't see her around.

Maximus: She's still at work.

Grandpa: How would you like to go to Grandma's and get something to eat? We can share with her a cup of tea and we can talk about this if you choose.

Maximus: That sounds good. I like Grandma's sandwiches.

As we walked outside, Grandpa asked me, "How was the game last night?"

Maximus: It was phenomenal, Grandpa, I enjoyed all of it: warming up, the game, and celebrating the victory afterwards. It was a great time. I felt joy for those five hours. I love that. I scored, I defended, I encouraged my team, and I enjoyed the cheers, and enjoyed the victory. I have been thinking seriously about making a career in sports.

Grandpa: What's stopping you? What are you waiting for?

Maximus: I don't know, Grandpa, I don't want to quit school either. I am not a quitter, but they just... They don't get it.

Grandpa: What don't they get, son?

Maximus: They don't get that I've been working hard all year and it is only fair that I just pass on to the next grade.

Grandpa: How did you get to this position?

Maximus: I told you, Grandpa, they're just not fair.

Grandpa: You're saying that they did this to you?

Maximus: Of course they did. I know they blame it on me.

Grandpa: Son, look at us. Where are we now?

Maximus: We are at the front door of your house.

Grandpa: Where were we before now?

Maximus: We were at my house.

I answered and I knew something was coming my way. Grandpa took my arm and led me to sit on a bench against the exterior of his house. As he sat me down, and he sat next to me, he turned slightly toward me and he looked me in the eye and said, *"Now is the product of the past and the foundation of the future.* We are where we are today because of the decisions we made in the past. We arrived at this exact point because of the route we took when we left your house. We could have taken a different route and that would have gotten us here earlier or later. The route we chose could have helped us or worked against us. We could have left your house earlier and that would also have impacted the time we took to make it here. We are here, at this specific moment, as a result. Results do not lie. We can choose to ignore them, but that does not make them go away. The wise person is the one who knows that results are the best indicators of where he is now and what kind of decisions he has made that led him to where he is. I pride myself for having such a wise grandchild and I know you just needed a little time to reflect on this matter. Now here's my question for you, son: Who made us take the route we took from your house to here?"

Maximus: No one, Grandpa. That's the route we normally take and I think we took it without even thinking about it.

Grandpa: That's true. So who took the route?

Maximus: We did.

Grandpa: That's right. We chose that route, even if it was unintentional or based on habits, we still chose the route that got us here.

Maximus: I need to think about that, Grandpa.

Grandpa: *Thinking is your first step to excellence.* While you do the thinking, I will check with Grandma about what she has for us to nibble on for the evening. How does that sound?

I remember Grandpa gave me time to think, as I had requested. He came back after several minutes, saying, "Grandma said it will be a couple more minutes before she has something for us. She said she has a treat for you and it is worth waiting for."

"Thank you, Grandpa. I have a question for you. How is it possible that I am the only one responsible for this result? Why are they not as responsible as I am, or even more?"

"Because you are the ultimate decision maker for how well, or how badly, you do in any area of *your* life. No one will know the exact thoughts you have in your mind. No one will know the exact emotions you feel inside. Others may suggest or even push certain routes your way. However, only you can decide which route to take. That route will determine the result you achieve. Therefore, you decide the results you will achieve. Blaming is a loser's game. If you find yourself blaming anyone or anything for the results you have, then it is time for a quick fix. There is a truly quick, easy and powerful way to fix it."

I remember not having enough courage to ask about the way to "fix it." I remember sitting quiet for a few minutes, staring at the ground as I held my hands together, with my elbows on my thighs, and leaned forward. Grandpa, of course, did not volunteer the answer and so I asked, "What is the quick way, Grandpa?"

"Come with me, I'll show you." Grandpa grabbed my arm to walk me to the house. We went straight to his room, and he opened the door to a dark space, guiding me to the side of the room where he had his armoire. He positioned me in the middle. Then he stepped behind me, gently grabbed my shoulders and gently guided me to face the mirror of the armoire and said, "Take your time. Talk to that guy for as long as you need. I'll be waiting outside with your treat that your grandma promised when you are done. No rush. This is very important."

He turned the lights on as he walked outside out of the room and shut the door. I looked at myself in the mirror for a few minutes, trying to understand this concept that my grandfather was trying to teach me. For a few minutes I couldn't see anything but my body standing in front of the mirror and the rest of the furniture in the room. At the same time, something was playing again and again in my head—it was what Grandpa had said about how results don't lie.

As I looked at myself in the mirror, I felt numb. Everything else I saw reflecting in the mirror disappeared. I did not see anything in that mirror except myself. The entire background became transparent; I was the only one existing in that environment. I looked even deeper and found my focus. I looked into my own eyes. I found myself walking closer to the mirror. I remember the train of thoughts and the emotional rollercoaster that was inside of me. It didn't take me long to realize that being in an unfavorable position to pass to the next grade was a result. That result was the outcome of certain routes I had taken. I found myself thinking that I spent a lot of time with my friends because they wanted me to. I remember thinking I did a lot of things for the house, for my mother, and for many other people, which took me away from doing my homework. I also remember thinking that all of these things were obligations that I needed to fulfill and that explained the routes that I had taken.

But I looked deeper into my own eyes in the mirror and I remembered what my grandfather had told me just a few minutes before: *no matter what the external factors were, I was responsible for taking the routes I had chosen.* He was right. I made myself believe that taking care of all those external matters was an obligation of mine; however, in reality I wanted to make myself think that way so I could justify my actions. In reality I wanted to do those things instead of my schoolwork.

I felt terrible. How could I think this way, behave this way, and live this way? It was a moment of truth that I needed. I felt that I needed to think even more and dig deeper into my actions. However, I felt a mountain of disappointment and disapproval about myself.

I kept repeating to myself, *How could I?* How could I think the way I did? Not me—I knew better; I learned to think, yet I didn't. Apparently it took me longer than my grandfather had expected. He didn't have the heart to break my train of thought so he sent Grandma to check on me.

"Honey, your treat is waiting and it will be cold if you don't come now. Can't you smell it?" I gathered myself quickly, took a deep breath and turned around in respect for my grandmother's presence. I smiled and answered, "Of course, Grandma, I bet the neighborhood can smell it, too."

I came out of the room to find the small circular wooden table that my grandmother always used when she prepared something for me. There were two chairs at the table and my Grandpa took one and put the other one facing him. The tray on the table had two plates. A small plate had one sandwich and a bigger plate held four sandwiches.

"I just finished making the bread, and it's really hot so be careful. My cousin brought us fresh honey from the farm today and I know how much you love that. There you go, your fresh honey and fresh homemade butter and fresh homemade bread as you like it. I don't want to see anything left."

"Thank you, Grandma," I said as I kissed her forehead and sat on the chair facing my grandfather, who was waiting for me to start eating. As I grabbed a sandwich to get the first bite, I remembered what had happened. Then I was lost again in my thoughts, trying to figure out what exactly happened, why, and how. And most importantly how I allowed myself to make the choices I made.

"This mint drink will freshen you up and change the taste," said Grandpa as he slid a small glass in front of me. He nodded his head as if he was signaling to me that he understood. He looked straight into my eyes, as he usually did, showing me that he was present and listening.

Maximus: I messed up, Grandpa. I took the wrong routes and I made bad choices. What is even worse is, I convinced myself that those choices were not my mistakes. For almost seven months I blamed the results on everyone else but the person who was responsible for those results: me. I was never this way, what happened? I have always been responsible, why am I taking a backseat? Why do I prefer to be in a victim state? Why did I forget that this leads to a powerless mindset? What worries me is that I did not even know that I was enjoying being a victim and having no power. If I had no power in my life then who would? It's my own life that is in this messy shape and I was content to do nothing about it but to blame someone else. What if that someone else was not ready or willing to do anything for me? What if they didn't care? What if they cared but that's what they wanted for me? How did I get in the position of disempowering myself and being content to be a victim? What is wrong with me?

Grandpa: You never cease to amaze me, son. You never cease to make me prouder every moment I look at you. You never cease to confirm your wisdom, awareness, courage in facing yourself, and freshness of your perspective. You have said a lot of things but I have one question for you: What are you left with, so far, to teach someone else in the world in your situation?

I took a deep breath, I leaned back against my chair and I put my sandwich down. "I don't know, Grandpa. I don't know. All that I can think about is how I gave up on myself."

"See what you did? You even pushed away his appetite. Are you happy now that he's not even finishing his first sandwich?" Grandma was sitting on a mattress on the floor preparing her favorite tea for the evening. "Come on, honey, I have a phenomenal cup of tea made for you. It deserves your sweet baby lips. I will even give you another cup of tea, only to you and not to Grandfather. Please finish your sandwiches."

Maximus: But this is very important for me and Grandpa is teaching me how to be a wise man for myself, my family, my friends, and mankind. I seem to be far away from it now and it is time for me to learn.

Grandma: God bless you, son. I can almost swear you were born wise.

Grandpa: Grandma is right. Finish your sandwiches, enjoy your drink, and think of my question. We have all the time we need, my prince.

It was quite comforting to have the wisdom of the world in my grandfather and the love of the universe in my grandmother right by my side.

Two things kept repeating in my head: Grandpa's sayings, "Now is the product of the past" and "Blaming is a loser's game."

Maximus: I am not a loser, Grandpa. It is true that I blamed my circumstances on other people, but no more. I am responsible for what I have. I chose to be where I am now. I just need to know how to get back to my normal self and make the right decisions.

Grandpa: You already started the process. You already took the first two steps out of four. Step number one is to know that today's results are the product of past decisions. Step number two is to give up the blaming game and take ownership of your decisions. You must claim 100% responsibility for everything you have in life.

Maximus: I can't wait to know steps number three and four. I am truly anxious to change my circumstances. I am a winner and winners are always responsible. What is step number three, Grandpa?

Grandpa: You are already at step number three, my prince. You amazingly shifted from step two to step three with your last sentence. You are correct, my prince. Winners take responsibility and do not beat themselves up and stop at that point. As you came out of the room, until the moment before you spoke, you beat yourself up for everything that had happened. However, you quickly shifted to a higher position, the position of winners. You are absolutely correct, my prince. Winners take responsibility for 100% of everything they have. Responsibility is extremely different from beating oneself up or swimming in the victim pool. By taking responsibility, you claim ownership of your circumstances. You claim the ultimate power of choice that you have, and you declare your presence and empowerment to make a difference in every aspect of your life. That is the prince I know.

Maximus: Thank you, Grandpa. I know you are encouraging me so I can move on. I am ready to move on, so what is step number four?

Grandpa: Remember what I shared with you a few minutes ago when I said that now is the product of the past and the foundation of the future?

Maximus: I do remember that.

Grandpa: Excellent. What do you get out of that?

I thought for a couple of minutes. I wanted to make sure that I truly understood the concept of the wisdom that my grandfather was teaching me. I repeated to myself the exact words he had told me multiple times: Now is the product of the past and the foundation of the future. Now is the product of the past and the foundation of the future. I lifted my head, sat back against my chair, and took a deep breath with a phenomenal sense of accomplishment. With confidence I answered, "I know that where I stand today, good or bad, is the result of everything that happened in the past. Knowing that I cannot change the past, except my belief about it, leads me to believe that my only power to change anything would apply to my present and my future. Since I am not in the future and I am only in the present. I can construct my present circumstances and make powerful decisions that will serve as the foundation for the days to come in my future."

Grandpa: Here I was thinking that I have all the wisdom, while my prince just proved to me that the few years he has lived on this Earth are good enough to place him among the wise. I could have not put it any better, my son. Now it is my turn to ask a question: what is the next step?

Maximus: I need to sit down with myself, review and understand the decisions I have made and where I misjudged the outcome. Once I understand that, I will move on to the next step. I already see the next step. It is as clear as a blue sky at the dawn of a beautiful spring day. I am not repeating this class. I am not lagging behind. I will not wait on the bench for the next bus. I am not going to watch life pass me by while I ignore my responsibility and disempower myself. I am going to pass this grade. I am passing this grade as of this moment, Grandpa. That is my goal. I have two and half months to achieve it. I need to have a concise plan to get there. I have to go, Grandpa. I have to go.

I stood up and kissed Grandpa on his forehead. I kneeled to reach my grandmother's forehead to kiss it and thanked her for the sandwiches. I ran out of my grandparents' house to my house. On my way to my house I could see nothing but the paper and pen that I was going to use to analyze and understand why and how I had made my decisions so I could avoid making them again. If I had God's power at that moment I would have just folded the ground in front of me so I could make it to my house faster and start my planning.

I finally made it home. I sat down and wrote and wrote and wrote to confirm my initial conclusion. It was absolutely, with no shred of a doubt, my own decisions that had gotten got me to where I was. The school, the teachers, my friends, the Boy Scouts—no one else in the world had any impact on my decisions. I looked at my grades from the first and the second quarters. I calculated the passing grade that I needed for the third quarter. I looked at the timeframe of 10 weeks; I started laying out my steps for each week to achieve my goal.

For the next 10 weeks I proved to myself that I was better than an outstanding student. I made up my mind that I would grasp everything that was said in class. It was very difficult to grasp everything since I had not made much effort for the previous seven months. However, I knew that would be the scenario, and my solution was to redo the class work when I got home. My days started at 3 AM and ended at 10 PM, every day for 10 weeks. No breaks, no days off, no soccer games, no hanging out, with only one goal in mind: to understand everything so I could ace my exams.

My mathematics teacher told me, as he handed me one of the tests that I took in the beginning of those 10 weeks, that I would not pass the grade even if I made a miracle happen. I remember that I magically did not hear what he said in my heart or my mind. I remember the words but they had absolutely no impact on me. I was focused and I had no doubt that I was going to achieve my goal. It was a stretch. It was kind of a dream. But I learned from my grandfather to dream big.

I set my goal to ace all of my exams no matter what the material was, no matter what the circumstance was, and no matter how big the challenge was. Ten weeks passed and then it was the 11th week. Exams week. I had tremendous confidence and a sense of empowerment that it was just a matter of taking the tests and success would be mine. And the rest is history.

Maximus smiled and looked around to see who was still awake. But before he even finished he heard Karam ask, "Grandpa... What happened next? Did you pass?"

The other children joined in, "You can't leave us hanging. Tell us, Grandpa... Pleeeeease!"

Maximus smiled and asked, "How could you have doubt in your grandfather's ability? Don't I deserve more of your faith?"

"Of course we do, Grandpa. It is different when we hear it from you. Please finish the story," said Aban.

"To tell you the truth the result was disappointing."

"Oh, no. I'm sorry, Grandpa. You didn't pass," said Karam.

"Well... not quite. I aced only nine exams out of ten."

"Yay! You passed! I knew you would. You, Grandpa, are the smartest man I know. I had no doubt," said Aidan.

"Thank you, my prince. My goal was to ace all of them but I missed by one. It is true that I passed, however, and at that time I had no doubt that I would pass. It was about achieving the goal that I set for myself and not the goal that the school set for me. I was grateful for the experience, and I still am. What I learned from the experience was more powerful and valuable than just passing to another grade. It took effort to learn and understand the concept: that now is the product of the past and the foundation of the future. It was thanks to my grandfather that I learned to take 100% responsibility and to own my circumstances. This was the first step toward my successful life: knowing that I was the only and ultimate responsible force behind my circumstances and life results. It was very empowering to understand what I had in me, *the power of choice*. It was also very important to learn not to beat myself up about what had happened, but to learn from it and quickly move on to the next step: the step of building today as the foundation of the future.

"Now my princes and princesses, this is the best part. It is time for me to get paid for telling you the story and I have the pleasure to decide how to get paid. How about a swim at the North Shore under the beautiful moonlight? Who are the brave souls to come with me?"

Maximus' question served as a trigger for the boys to stand up, form their circle and move in their regular happy circular dance, singing "We are all in and no one is out, we are all in and no one is out!" Laughter and joy filled the air and as they started walking toward the beach Aidan grabbed Maximus' hand and said, "I wish I met my great-grandfather, Grandpa. He was an extraordinary man and I am proud to be his great-grandson. I know how much you loved him and I love him, too."

"I wish you met him, too," said Maximus as he sat down on the beach, and he pulled Aidan closer to him while he kissed Aidan's head. As they both looked onto the moonlight in the ocean, Aidan laid on the sand, his head against his grandfather's thigh, with both his hands together on his little belly as he inhaled a deep breath and said, "I actually meet him every day through you, Grandpa. I am fortunate to be your grandson. Thank you for being my grandfather."

Maximus was deeply touched and could not even speak. He held his breath, worried his emotions would show in his voice. Tears rolled down his cheeks to meet the moonlight. He closed his eyes, thanking his grandfather for the wisdom that had made him valuable to his family, his friends, and mankind.

⌘ ⌘ ⌘

To shift your life and achieve your dreams practice the pillars of total ownership:

- *Every time you feel like blaming, look in the mirror.*
- *Don't beat yourself up. Just take responsibility.*
- *The present is the product of the past and the foundation of the future.*
- *You can control only this moment that will shape your future. What are you going to do to shape your life?*

The Wisdom of the Mine Worker

Distance is not what keeps you from your destiny.
It is your first step toward it.

"That was something last night, wasn't it?" asked Nagnag.

"Here we go again. Pain in the neck. The worst thorn in my side... my unwelcomed and hidden life partner. It was. I enjoyed it very much," whispered Maximus as he looked around him to make sure no one had heard him.

Nagnag: Come on now, Mr. Big Dreams. You asked me to give you some privacy and I did. You asked me to give you a break and I did, although you offended me when you said it was family time. I never thought of myself as an outsider, but that's okay. I have been nice to you for the last few days. So what's the attitude about?

Maximus: I know you don't just show up for nothing. You have been quite good at challenging me, to say the least, and I grew to learn that your presence means nagging more than anything else. So what do you want now?

Nagnag: You keep preaching that gratitude is one of the most common human traits. How about the times I supported you and I stayed by your side? What about the times that I challenged you and encouraged you to do even better and become even more powerful? I get no credit for that?

Maximus: Hurricanes bring rain and water, among other things. While water is good for the plants, for the ground and for humans, its excess is damaging to all of them. The sun is necessary for all beings, however excessive heat can be damaging to all of them.

Nagnag: My good friend, as you are the only one, and my life partner, I would never choose anyone besides you. I am grateful for such a powerful analogy. You raise me up to such valuable beings such as water and sun and I will happily take that as a compliment.

Maximus: Suit yourself. Whatever makes you happy.

Nagnag: I remember those days that you talked to the family about last night.

Maximus: You never stopped before that time and during the 10 weeks of my transformation to plant self-doubt in me. You even told me during the 11th week, when I was taking the tests, that I did everything I could and it was time to relax. You even had the audacity to tell me that if I didn't pass it would have been the fault of the teachers who graded my exams. You were a nightmare.

Nagnag: And you were stubborn. So how likely do you think your son, Muheeb, learned from the story you shared? I know you told the story because of how he managed the trip yesterday.

Maximus: Muheeb is action-oriented. I am not denying the value of planning. I am just showing the value of taking action.

Nagnag: I can't believe you just said that. You are justifying your son's shortcomings and lack of planning as a winner's behavior. That goes against what you have been teaching for the last 40 years. How biased, emotional, and unlike you is that?

Maximus: That's not what I said. Hold on, we're getting close to the resort and everybody is singing the returning song, so we can continue this battle later. I have a song to sing with my family now.

Aidan and Karam grabbed Maximus' hands while they jumped up and down trying to get their grandfather's attention. He had a huge smile on his face as he jumped up and down with them and started the troop's returning home song.

Come and see, come and see

What we learned from the tree

How we partnered with the open sea

And how we keep our spirit free

Come and see, come and see.

They danced around in a big circle, joining hands, jumping up and down, bowing and standing up, and then moving in a circular motion to start all over again. Elektra, Leila, Maximus' mother and their friends welcomed the troops home by clapping and standing up to bow in respect of their accomplishment. They helped everyone take off their backpacks as the children enthusiastically shared with them the special moments they had enjoyed over the prior two days.

"All right boys and girls, we have big plans for you tonight, so why don't you go ahead, freshen up and get some rest. A nice dinner will be ready for you when you come out."

Come and see, come and see

What we learned from the tree

How we partnered with the open sea

And how we keep our spirit free

Come and see, come and see.

The children sang and danced again. They made everyone laugh with their silliness and their love for life.

It was dinnertime. Elektra rang the bell that she had used for 20 years to call the children and grandchildren. She had brought the bell with her because she knew that it would be her moment of joy, a way to recall the old days. Her daughter Leila was inspired enough to have her own bell at home. As everyone gathered around a 12-foot table, the children grabbed their forks and spoons, banging on their plates, signaling their hunger and calling for action.

"Not yet, everyone. Uncle Omar and his family are on the way, let's be a little patient," said Leila.

Maximus took advantage of the time to teach the grandchildren one of his old Boy Scout songs.

Treat us with your gifts our skilled chef

We are on standby, we are on standby

After a full day

Of joy and play

Our bellies feel grey

And hearts of hunger sway

And we are still on standby, we are still on standby.

The children repeated the lyrics after him, as, banging the plates even harder and faster with their forks and spoons. That was a joyful moment for Maximus. He couldn't stop himself from standing and calling the grandchildren to follow him as he danced around the food table singing the song. He held his fork in his left hand and his spoon in his right, alternating both of them up and down with his steps. The children followed his footsteps and went around and around like a steam train, singing:

Treat us with your gifts our skilled chef

We are on standby, we are on standby

After a full day

Of joy and play

Our bellies feel grey

And hearts of hunger sway

And we are still on standby, we are still on standby. Again,

Treat us with your gifts our ...

Soon, everyone in the family joined the dance around the table, and Maximus' mother cheered their joy and their spirit. Omar, his wife and his daughter joined the end of the moving circle, repeating whatever they could catch from the song. Omar and his family had been part of Maximus' family for quite a while, and had learned that such behavior was an open invitation to whoever was willing to join. Then the food was brought to the table to break their enthusiasm for singing and give more empowerment to their bellies.

"This is the most delicious meal I have ever eaten in my entire life," said Aban.

"That must be a very, very long life," said Aidan, and everyone laughed.

"I don't see Amir. Did you leave him behind?" asked Elektra.

"He said he would join us later," answered Omar.

A minute later Maximus whispered to Omar, "You have never had a poker face. Even if you did, your voice betrays it every time. Is he all right?"

"He said he would come by later and spend some time with you. You'll tell me afterward if he is all right," answered Omar. He did not lift his eyes from his plate.

At the table, the adults enjoyed the dinner and tried to stretch it out as much as possible, to engrave it in their minds for times to come. The younger generation that gathered lived in the moment. They didn't fully understand how precious this moment was, but they were fortunate to be surrounded by adults who made the moments count.

"To the moments in our lives that make us unique, united and unbreakable," said Maximus.

"To the people who bring joy to our lives and make those moments exist," replied Omar.

"And to the chef who made my tummy sing tonight," said Karam, as she devoured a gigantic piece of chocolate cake, making everyone laugh.

"To our creator who blessed us with a long breadth of life to enjoy these moments," said Maximus' mother.

Amir arrived. "There he is, the prince of the island. It is wonderful to see you, son. Oh my, you have grown so much very fast," said Maximus as he stood up to give Amir a hug. "Come here, son, sit next to me. I missed you. May I please have a chair here?"

"It is good to see you. Make me proud and finish this, please," said Elektra as she piled food in a large oval plate and handed it to Amir.

"Thank you, thank you. I feel so special already. I miss you guys, too. It has been a while."

"Indeed, it has, brother. You never came to visit no matter how many times we invited you," said Maher.

"I promise I will. It's just... life, you know."

"Be sure you leave room for dessert. We have a full menu. We have lemon pie, triple chocolate cake, tiramisu, and fruit cocktail besides the sweet drinks. And if you have anything else in mind, I will make it for you," said Elektra.

It was an hour later when Amir was still struggling with the huge oval plate that Elektra had given him.

Omar announced that he was going home to get a few hours of sleep so he could be ready for the next day's work. As he stood up, Amir stood up as well, saying, "I'll drive you home, guys."

"No, no, no, son. I have not had enough of you and I'm not sure when my next moment with you will come so you're a hostage tonight. You're staying with me," said Maximus.

"He's all yours, my friend. I have no doubt he will be thrilled," Omar said.

Amir spoke up, "Let me help you with the bags at least. I see Aunt Elektra is sending you home with a week's worth of food."

"Let me help. I need to stretch," said Maximus as he grabbed one of the bags and headed toward Omar's minivan. "How's life treating you, son?" He waved to Omar and his family as they left the parking lot.

"I'm not sure, Uncle Maximus. I am still trying to figure that out," said Amir with a long sigh.

Maximus: You know that we spend most of our lives doing that, right? It is quite normal to have those moments and experience the feelings associated with them.

Amir: Discomfort can hang on for quite some time. It is discomforting hanging out with discomfort.

Maximus: I always liked your sense of humor and creativity in playing with words. Acknowledging discomfort as a stage, versus an uncontrollable lifestyle, is a skill. You are already ahead of many men and women in this life. It is a great start. So how long have you been at this stage?

Amir: For about 14 months.

Maximus: I applaud you for being specific. That is a huge indication of how responsible and ready you are for the next stage.

Amir: I am beyond ready. I just don't know what is next or how to get there.

Maximus: That's very much unlike you. You always knew what you wanted to do and what you wanted to be. I am certain you still have it in you. What has changed?

Amir: It is part of my frustration, Uncle. I always knew what I wanted, it just seems foggy right now and I don't know why.

Maximus: If you had to take a guess, what do you think the reason might be?

Amir: That's what my father asked me and he told me that you would ask me the same question. I don't want to guess. I want to know.

Maximus: Your persistence is empowering and admirable. In many cases we don't know, simply because it is the future. It is unknown by design. Other times we think we don't know simply because it is uncomfortable to know. We may have to be accountable and we may have to hold ourselves responsible. It is not critical at this point to know which one; it is critical to actually embark on the beginning of "the knowing" path. If you were to take a wild guess into why you don't know, what would that be?

It took Amir took a couple of minutes to answer the question as they were walking back toward the dinner area. On the way, Maximus found a bench by a light fixture so he decided to give Amir some more time to think. As Amir exhaled a long sigh, he sat down next to Maximus and said, "I can think of more than one guess."

Maximus: Excellent. I am all ears.

Amir: One of the possible guesses is uncertainty. I am not certain if what I want to do is achievable. Even if it was achievable, and I don't know that, it makes me feel disempowered because I wouldn't know how to achieve it. Another possible guess is lack of confidence. I often think of the possibility of not making it to where I want to be, and how that would make me feel. I wonder what kind of impact that would have on my life. I don't want to be responsible for decisions that I make today that may impact me negatively in the future. I am sure I would not be happy with it.

Maximus: You're saying that if you decided to take an action today that you would be responsible for its outcome in the future. What about if you decided not to take an action, who would be responsible?

Amir: I am responsible. What's wrong with me? It is obvious that not making a decision is a decision by itself. So either way I will be making a decision and I will ultimately be responsible for it.

Maximus: Bravo! You're rocking as usual. Which one would you rather be responsible for?

Amir: If I take an action and make a decision I will still have respect for myself, versus allowing circumstances to dictate my life and indecisiveness to drive me to victimize myself and feel disempowered. Of course making a decision sounds better. I'm still uncertain though.

Maximus: It is quite normal to be uncertain. The future is the father of uncertainty. By the way, I always meant to ask you this question but I never had a chance; let me ask you now. How did you manage to build a soccer team that was ranked second in its region while located on an island with very few resources?

Amir: That was ranked second in its region? That was during my teenage years. I can't believe you still remember that.

Amir smiled and leaned back against the bench, lifting both of his arms and shoulders, resting them against the edge of the bench, then he lifted his head toward the stars and continued, "That was a great time. I had a lot of passion for soccer. I always thought about just one thing all the time: enjoying the game. I didn't care if our team was ranked at the top or the bottom. I believed that we would be a great team as long as we shared expectations and goals, and we did. It was not easy to find 16 soccer players, let alone highly skilled soccer players, but we shared the same beliefs and same passion. I knew we would be exceptional. I just knew we would make it."

Maximus: It's great to see your beautiful smile, son. Your face lit up as you were talking about that. I don't think we need this lamplight anymore.

Amir: Thank you, Uncle. I wouldn't go that far, though.

Maximus: You repeated a theme in your last description few times. You were keen on believing.

Amir: I guess belief overcame uncertainty and my lack of confidence back then. Are you saying that's what I lack right now?

Maximus: I'm not saying anything, son. You are saying everything.

Amir: I am, indeed. The more I think about it now, the clearer it becomes. I believed back then.

Maximus: Tell me more about that belief. How far did it go?

Amir: It filled my heart and soul. I felt it with all my senses. I had zero doubt we would achieve our goal. I heard the people chanting in the stadium. I smelled the grass of the field. I saw us triumphing and excelling in our games. I tasted victory on my lips. I hugged my peers and touched their faces as we celebrated at the end of every game. I saw it all waiting for us. It was that simple, Uncle.

Maximus: That simple, hmm?

Amir: It's amazing... It was that simple.

Maximus: How long did it take you guys to achieve your goals?

Amir: We were ranked second in the region two years after starting our team. However, every time we played a game we felt we were closer to achieving our ultimate goal.

Maximus: What is your ultimate goal right now?

Amir: I feel I have many and I can't make up my mind.

Maximus: Which one do you think is the most important?

Amir: I don't know. They are all important.

Maximus: How willing are you to play the "what if" game like we used to do in the old days?

Amir: I'd like that. I am ready.

Maximus: Great. This time it may be a little direct and tough. How prepared are you?

Amir: I'm your man. Try me.

Maximus: Imagine that tonight was the last night of your life, and that you had an angel come down to you from the skies to give you one more opportunity in life. He tells you that he is at your service with all the power in the world, with all resources at your disposal, with one caveat: you must have only one thing to accomplish before you leave this world and it must be completed before sunrise. What would that one thing be that would make you satisfied to accomplish it before leaving forever?

Amir: I would establish a program that would benefit teenagers. The program would help them make better decisions early in life so they would be ahead of the game and live their dream life with less sacrifices and trade-offs.

Maximus: Impressive.

Amir: It has been a dream of mine for a long time.

Maximus: The dream is impressive. What is equally impressive is how quickly you answered and how certain you were when answering the question. What would achieving that goal bring to you?

Amir: Oh, Uncle... I can only imagine the face of a 17-year-old boy feeling that he has found all the answers, or the system that would help him find the answers, to all of his mind-boggling questions. What a wonderful accomplishment to have him find himself and figure out his life purpose early so he could achieve it, live it, and enjoy it. I could never ask for a better legacy that would impact the world this way in my absence.

Maximus: A noble role for a noble man. I can only congratulate you and the generations to come for such an accomplishment. I forgot to tell you that the angel will do only the things you tell him to do. He has to hear your requests because he can't read your mind. You would be provided all the powers and resources that you ask for but you have to do the thinking and the planning. What would you do?

Amir: I don't know. It is such a short period of time.

Maximus: Have you ever heard the story of Andy the mineworker from your father?

Amir: No, I don't recall such a thing.

Maximus: I would like you to ask your father about the story and let's meet tomorrow at dawn so we can enjoy the virgin swim of the day as we used to do years ago. Remember that?

Amir: I have not done it for a while and I miss it. That's a great plan. I will walk you to your room.

Maximus: Hey! I'm not that old, you know. I can still take care of myself and whoever comes my way, even if he is as young, vigorous, and unbeatable as you. (Smiling)

Amir: Of course, Uncle. I would not cross your path either. I enjoyed our talk very much. I will see you first thing in the morning. Have a good night.

Maximus: Sweet dreams.

Amir strolled toward his house, thinking about the conversation he had with Maximus. When he arrived home, he saw the kitchen light go on. He realized that his father was waking up to prepare for his workday. Amir entered the house softly so he wouldn't disturb the sleepers' peace. He made his way to the kitchen to find his father.

Amir: Good morning, Dad. How did you sleep?

Omar: I slept all right. Have you slept yet?

Amir: No, not yet.

Omar: How did you leave your Uncle Maximus?

Amir: We had a long conversation that I enjoyed very much. I always enjoy my conversations with Uncle Maximus. Talking to him was enlightening, empowering, and relaxing. He asked me a very important question to ask you.

Omar: Uh-oh, he has set me up. I hope I have an answer for you.

Amir: He asked me if I had ever heard the story of Andy the mineworker. Would you please share it with me? Uncle Maximus indicated that you know the story. That was his assignment for me before I meet him for the virgin swim of the day.

Omar: Lucky you, the first waves of the day! Well, Andy was a 19-year-old boy who lived in a very small town where everybody knew everybody. Everyone in that little town worked in the town's mine. Andy was responsible for his father, who had been injured working at the mine and was disabled. Andy also took care of his mother and his three sisters. Working in the mine was not his dream. He had always wanted to be an airplane pilot. But because Andy never left the small town, he viewed his life as being only as big as the mine. He wondered, if he walked far enough in the mine, whether he would find the other side of the world, the world of unlimited possibilities, where he could learn to be a pilot.

One day, Andy decided to walk to the other side of the mine. He wondered if he would find daylight toward the end of the mine—as light would indicate an opening to the other world. He had no idea how long it would take to get there, but he had a burning desire and a belief that there was something there. He wished that he had a device that would show him the end of the tunnel. He wished that there were a mode of transportation that would carry him there quickly to see if the opening existed. If it didn't exist, he could make it back quickly so no one would notice and he would not waste much time.

He said to himself, "I can wonder, wish, and remain here without knowing or I can go and find out." He decided to go but something crossed his mind. He had nothing but the little lamp attached to his helmet to show him the way. That lamp did not project light more than six feet ahead. Andy told himself, "I can either stay here because I can't see more than six feet ahead at a time, or I can go six feet at a time and see what comes up."

He was not prepared to give up, which made the choice clear to him. He decided to take his journey, being able to see only six feet at a time, to reach his goal. Andy left all the money he had underneath his pillow for his mother to find in case he took too long to come back. He gathered food in his pockets and packed a little container that he normally took with him for lunch, and brought some water. He decided not to share his intentions with anyone.

Andy walked in the mine, nonstop, for hours. Each time he took a step, he saw six feet ahead of him. He realized that as long as he kept moving toward his goal, the path would be revealed. He also realized that when he stopped, the light stopped, and he couldn't see more than the six feet that he already saw. He became determined that stopping was not an option. It was mesmerizing how quickly he could see the rest of the tunnel by just taking one step at a time.

Nearly 16 hours later, to his surprise and amusement, he saw a glimpse of light. He wasn't sure it was anything more than his imagination. About 20 minutes later, Andy saw a much bigger light source that confirmed to him that it had not been his imagination and that there really was an opening on the other side of the tunnel. With great enthusiasm and excitement, he ran toward the light. As he came out of the tunnel, he quickly realized that it was not a different world. It was still his small town, just seen from the other side. While his hopes were crushed by not finding another world—the world of possibilities—he realized that he actually had found the world of opportunities. He found it inside of him. He learned that no matter how hard, far, ambiguous, and uncertain the goal was, he would make it.

"Makes sense. Makes sense," whispered Amir. He was staring at his hands as if he was trying to see the path in the lines of his palms.

Omar: What makes sense?

Amir: It makes sense that Uncle Maximus wanted me to know about Andy the mineworker.

Omar: That's only half of the story, son. I will leave the pleasure of sharing the other half to your Uncle Maximus. It's time for both of us to go. The birds are singing to the daylight coming out. Let's go, I'll give you a ride.

Amir: Thank you, Dad, but I'll walk to the resort. I need the time to think.

"Makes sense," said Omar, smiling as he tapped Amir's shoulder.

Amir: How did you sleep, Uncle Maximus?

Maximus: Not enough, but okay. How about you?

Amir: Not yet. I just can't wait for the virgin swim. By the way, why do you guys call it that?

Maximus: I take full responsibility for the name. I think of the waves of early-morning as newborns. They are pure without any stain or impurity and I find them cleansing and refreshing so I call them the virgin waves. Over time the name became the virgin swim. Are you ready to be purified?

Amir: Let's do this.

Maximus: What a treat! Thank you God for this blessing.

Amir: It is indeed refreshing, Uncle. Thank you for this phenomenal idea.

Maximus: You live on the island; why don't you do this every day?

Amir: I used to until my mind took me to the uncertainty island where nothing is virgin.

Maximus: Did you get a chance to talk to your father?

Amir: I was lucky to catch him eating his breakfast before going to work and he was very kind to share such a beautiful story with me. That was a great suggestion, Uncle.

Maximus: What did you learn?

Amir: That I don't have to see every single step all the way to where I need to be. All I need is to see far enough ahead so that I can keep progressing toward my destiny. Six feet ahead every time he took a step is quite powerful.

Maximus: Now how will that work for you?

Amir: I have not gotten that far yet. I know I need to create a legacy that will impact the world. Maybe I need to make a plan like Andy did.

Maximus: What are you waiting for?

Amir: I was hoping to do that with you. You make it all seem possible.

Maximus: Thank you for the confidence, son. That is overwhelmingly satisfying. So let me ask you this question: Remember that angel that I told you about last night?

Amir: Of course I do.

Maximus: He was there only for the night and he couldn't wait any longer. He had to go and take his powers with him but he had full confidence in your powers. So now, with your brainpower, what would be your next move?

Amir: I need a plan. I need to have a path to walk. It is not important that I see all the details right now. What is important is to know there is a path and I can see far enough to keep walking toward my goal.

Maximus: Great. I'm listening. Tell me about it.

Amir: A pen and a paper would be helpful, so let me go and grab them from the reception desk.

Maximus: Didn't you just say that you need to see just far enough? So why are you going all the way there? What I asked you was: What can you do with what you have right now?

Amir: I guess I can use my finger in the sand.

Maximus: There you go. Now what?

Amir: I need to do a study and collect as much information as possible on the most common challenges teenagers have. Such as, what questions they ask themselves and their peers; obstacles they seem to face when they are soul-searching; common thoughts and emotions they face that encourage them or hinder them as they proceed to the next step; and common desires and dreams and where they come from. Questions are racing into my head that I can't even keep up with. I need to write this down.

Maximus: So let's call this step searching and analysis. And let's assume that you have the results of your search and the details of your analysis, what's next?

Amir: I... I don't know. Is it bad that I don't know?

Maximus: It is actually normal, because all you can see right now is six feet ahead. The six-feet-ahead method is a phenomenal way to get you started, place your heart in the right spot, and stabilize your feet to launch. It is also effective to boost your morale and maintain your faith to keep going. What would make the six-feet-ahead method even more powerful is the BMBS method.

Amir: BMBS? What is that?

Maximus: That is Breakthrough, Medium, Baby goals with Set dates. You already have your breakthrough goal. That is your destination. You are where you are today: at the beach enjoying the virgin swim with your Uncle Maximus and having your first thoughts about your research and analysis. First you set your medium-range goals. Those goals will act as miniature breakthrough goals in comparison to where you are at the moment. Each of them will signal to you how close you are to your breakthrough goal. You may have as many medium-range goals as necessary to enforce your belief that you are on the right path to your breakthrough goal.

Between every two medium-range goals you will have baby goals. Baby goals are tiny victories that you achieve more frequently, daily or weekly but no longer than biweekly. Baby goals are logical steps to get you from one medium-range goal to another. They are filled with tremendous energy and pure productivity. Achieving your baby goals will raise your confidence and willpower every hour of every day you live, proceeding to your destiny. How does that sound?

Amir: Acceptable and soon will be manageable, once I am able to put them down on paper so I can see my steps from now toward my goal.

Maximus: Since you definitely have to have the pen and paper, I will let you make the trip to the reception desk while I have a peaceful conversation with my newcomers, the virgin waves.

After several minutes, Maximus walked to the shore to find Amir surrounded with papers and immersed in writing. Without disturbing him, he laid down next to him on the sand enjoying the first rays of sunshine of the day on his nicely aged body. It was peaceful enough that he took a good nap. When he awoke, Amir had disappeared. Maximus stood up and took a good look in the water. It was still early and no one was swimming. Then he saw Amir running toward him like an unstoppable train.

Maximus: You have not slept in two days! Where did you get this energy?

Amir: From clarity. I have not felt this clear, this powerful, this focused, this confident, this successful, this rich, this free, this inspirational, this determined since I was 17. I feel I can take on the world, and more.

Maximus: It is refreshing to see you back. Now there are a couple things that will make the process even more powerful.

Amir: Bring it on, Uncle. I am unstoppable!

Maximus: What may stop you at any point from reaching your breakthrough goal?

Amir: Nothing. I got it, Uncle.

Maximus: Your confidence is very much appreciated. Think harder. What are the external and internal factors that may stop you from continuing or delaying you?

Amir: I suppose financial reasons, lack of support, maybe, and self-doubt. Any factor may show up and may potentially stop me or delay me.

Maximus: How likely is it that any of these factors, or others, will stop you or delay you from achieving your goals?

Amir: Practically, they may delay me, but nothing will stop me. I may get tired, or burned out, but I'll never give up.

Maximus: What is your strategy to make sure that the delay does not turn into giving up?

Amir: I am beyond that point, Uncle. I know where and what I need to be. I know what makes me feel fulfilled. I never want to lose what I feel now, ever again. I am framing this snapshot of time of my life so that I am never alive another day without feeling it. I know where I need to be. I know my path. I know my milestones. I know the six-feet-ahead method will ignite my belief torch if at any time it weakens or tends to go to sleep. The last eight hours have been transformational on all levels. I am back again. I am again Amir who is destined to impact his world beyond his imagination. I am the son of Omar who shifted his life upside down, 180°, between the time he knew that his wife was pregnant and the time his firstborn made it to this life. I have learned from the best and I have no excuse to fail or settle. My only option is to succeed in my mission and positively impact my life and the lives of everyone around me. My impact will reach the teenagers of today and tomorrow. It is my promise to you, to the world and to myself. It is my promise and I am a man of my word for only the men who live up to their promises deserve to triumph, lead and succeed!

Maximus pulled him against his chest, to hug him like he hugged his own children, and whispered, "You are the pride of your parents, your generation and the dreamers who share your passion. You are tremendous. You have made the day of an old man."

"Thank you, Uncle. I have always loved you like a father and you have never treated me less than a son. My father always told me that you knew me the longest, after him and my mother, as you met me when my mother was pregnant, without even meeting my mother."

"That was quite an experience. Thank God you're not as hardheaded as your father was when I met him. I don't even know if you would've accepted him as a father if you went back then," said Maximus as he laughed with Amir.

"Oh... One more thing, Uncle. When my father told me the story he finished by saying that whatever he told me was only half. He also said that he would leave to you the pleasure of telling me the other half."

"That was everything, son. I don't know what your father is talking about."

"I don't know either. I'll check with him when I get home."

"I would love to see you again before I head back to the city," Maximus said, "But don't worry about making it an obligation. I know you are on a quest and I am confident I will either see you soon or hear about you soon. Make your voice loud and clear. Get some rest."

Nagnag: Why didn't you tell him?"

Maximus: How is it your business?

Nagnag: It amazes me how you keep asking these questions. Everything in your head is my business. If you don't want it to be my business then don't think. It is as simple as that. Why didn't you tell him?

Maximus: It is my story and I can share it any way I choose with whomever I choose.

Nagnag: I doubt that you are embarrassed. I can guess what it is but I'd rather hear it from you.

Maximus: I wanted him to know on his own. It is part of the charm of the story.

Nagnag: How do you envision he would do that on his own?

Maximus: He knows my middle name is Andy and he's heard all the stories about my grandfather before. He is smart enough to figure it out on his own.

Nagnag: Where is the charm, exactly?

Maximus: It's in the suspense of telling the story, yet it is only half of the story. It is the legacy of telling that specific story.

Nagnag: Weird as usual, but what can I say? it's your story.

Maximus: I am glad you know that, you pain in the neck.

Nagnag: By the way... when are you going to write that book about your grandfather?

⌘ ⌘ ⌘

"If you fail to plan you plan to fail." –Benjamin Franklin-

Follow these planning principles to achieve:

- *Seeing one step ahead toward your destiny is all that you need to start your journey.*
- *BMBS method:*
    - *Specify your Breakthrough goals.*
    - *Break it into Medium-range goals.*

- o *Achieve your Baby goals first.*
- *Set dates (threshold and objective).*
- *Remember: It is your responsibility to put the plan into action.*

Meet Your Best Friend and

Your Worst Enemy

"Who never stumbles never learns to get up."
–Aboul Kacem Achebbi–

"Rise and shine, princes of the future, glorious life explorers. This is a new day in your lives that you don't want to let pass without making it count. Come on, let's go. The waves are calling your names. Hold on... Sorry, what did you say? You haven't seen Farris for a long time? You miss him? I'm sure he misses you, too. Hey Farris, come on, my prince. Did you hear the waves calling your name?"

"Just a little bit more, Grandpa. Tell them I'm coming. Just little bit more... sleep."

"My prince, the morning waves don't wait for anyone. They will come to glorify those who rise up to catch the first few breezes of the dawn and wash their bones with pure water that will energize them for the rest of the day. Come on, son. You are among the glorified, aren't you? Karam, Aidan, Aban, let's go."

"I'm ready, Grandpa. I was born ready," said Aidan as he rubbed his eyes with his fists in an effort to get himself up and running.

Maximus called, "Come on Farris, we'll have fun. That's my fearless leader. You got it, Aidan, I count on you to get the princes and princesses rolling on the road to enjoy the early morning."

"You got it, Grandpa. Come on, guys."

Maximus stepped outside and gathered a few bottles of water and towels for the children. He knew that once they reached the water they would be thirsty, hungry, and unstoppable. Aidan got everyone ready and called his grandpa.

"Excellent. Let's roll!" announced Maximus in his usual enthusiastic tone.

"Grandpa, are the morning waves too big? I am only four years old you know!"

"The early morning waves are unlike any others. They are the newborn waves of the day. Newborns are tiny, soft, and full of life, like you."

"What if I drown?"

"What makes you think you will drown?"

"I am only four."

"I am also four, and I won't drown," said Karam as she stomped the ground next to her grandfather. She couldn't wait to get to the water.As soon as they saw the majestic blue ocean the children ran toward it—except for Farris. He grabbed Maximus' right thumb with his hands and joined him for the walk to the shore. While the kids were splashing, jumping and diving into the water, Farris was still standing next to his grandpa on the shore. "Come on Farris, it feels so good. Come on!"

"Okay," said Farris as he put his right index finger between his teeth.

"Grandpa, can we go back to get my life vest? I can't swim without it," asked Farris as he tilted his head to see his grandfather's response.

"Of course we can do that, son. Where did you leave it?"

"I don't know, Grandpa. I can ask Mommy."

"Your mom and dad went hiking right before we came here and I don't think they will be back for a while. Do you think you can find it?"

"I don't know, Grandpa. We can try, but I don't want to miss the morning waves."

"That's a very valid concern, so what are we going to do?"

"I don't know, Grandpa. I am afraid I will drown if I swim without my life vest."

"What makes you think that, son?"

"Well... You know how on TV, when people drown and then they are given a life vest? I prefer to have my life vest before and not after."

"That's very smart thinking, my prince. Why did those people on TV drown?"

"No, they didn't drown but it was very embarrassing afterwards."

"Why do you say that?"

"After their lives were saved, they looked stupid. They could've just had their life vests from the beginning and saved themselves the embarrassment."

"Is that why you have to have your life vest before you go in?"

"Of course, Grandpa, I don't want my cousins to make fun of me. What if I don't make it and they laugh at me? I wouldn't like that," said Farris as he crossed his tiny arms, put his head down, and frowned.

"By the way, did I ever tell you what your name means?"

"I think you did, Grandpa, but I can't remember now."

"You remember what I gave you for birthday present last year?"

"Yes," said Farris enthusiastically, "it was a big black statue of a knight riding a beautiful horse and holding his sword high. I love that one, Grandpa!"

"I am glad you loved it, my prince. I know how much you love horses and I thought it would make you happy. But there was another reason I gave you that gift. Try to remember, I know you have it all in you."

It took Farris a few seconds to jump up and say, "Oh yes, I remember you telling me when I opened my gift, 'That is you.' What does that mean, Grandpa?"

Maximus: The name "Farris" is given to a strong man who has no fear in his heart and has no concerns about failing. A Farris is a very courageous, confident, and strong man, like you.

Farris: Yes, I remember that now, Grandpa. I also remember you telling me that I would be a Farris like no other.

Maximus: Indeed, my prince. You are a Farris like no other.

Farris: I don't feel I am a Farris right now.

Maximus: What do you mean, my prince? Once a Farris, always a Farris.

Farris: A Farris has no concern about failing. And I am concerned that I will drown and my cousins will laugh at me.

Maximus: Where did you learn these words? I never heard you use them before.

Farris: I hear them a lot on TV and I also hear my mom and dad. I often hear them saying, "How embarrassing is that!"

Maximus: What do you think that means?

Farris: It means other people make fun of you when you don't do something right.

Maximus: People like whom?

Farris: You know, Grandpa. People... like friends, neighbors, and other kids you play with.

Maximus: Farris, do you remember the story of the chicken eagle?

Farris: Yes, I do. That is the story of the eagle that grows up in a chicken nest and never learns to fly like an eagle.

Maximus: And do you remember why that was?

Farris: Yes. It was because everyone around him was a chicken and didn't know how to fly like eagles do, so they told him that he couldn't fly like an eagle. And every time he saw other eagles soaring freely in the sky he wanted to fly like them but never did. Because he was afraid that if he tried, he would fall and the other chickens would laugh at him and he would be a joke. So he spent his life as a chicken until he died.

Maximus: So are you a Farris or an eagle chicken?

Farris: What do you mean, Grandpa? I am Farris, did you forget?

Maximus: Never, my son, never. I named you Farris and I know you are a Farris. But, do you remember what we said about the name Farris: how it is strong, brave, and confident?

Farris: Yes, I do, Grandpa.

Maximus: Great. Do you remember what you said about the eagle chicken? How he was afraid of trying to fly and did not want to be embarrassed if he failed? So which one are you, Farris or the eagle chicken?

Farris: Of course I am Farris, Grandpa. I am never a chicken. I am brave, strong and confident.

Maximus: What was that...? I couldn't hear.

Farris: I am Farris, Grandpa. I am never a chicken. I am brave, strong and confident.

Maximus: Sorry, son. You are whispering, I can't hear you.

Farris: I am Farris, Grandpa. I am never a chicken. I am brave, strong and confident!

Maximus: Say again?

Farris: I am Farris, Grandpa. I am never a chicken. I am brave, strong and confident.

Maximus: And again, louder.

Farris: I am Farris, Grandpa! I am never a chicken! I am brave, strong and confident!

Maximus walked toward the water as he led Farris behind him. Farris repeated his answer, with gusto. "I am Farris, Grandpa. I am never a chicken. I am brave, strong and confident!" His cousins heard him and they came running toward him saying the same thing: "I am Farris, Grandpa. I am never a chicken. I am brave, strong and confident!" Maximus laughed with joy when he saw his grandchildren uniting, encouraging their young cousin. Farris hadn't known they would be so supportive. He gained his confidence and joined his cousins in celebration.

Maximus knew he still had some work to do. He had been able to teach adults and empower them to overcome fears of failure and to gain control over their emotions and future. However, that had not been done with enough rigor for children of Farris' age. He knew it would be very challenging to do that for a large group of children. He had to think of a way to ensure that the message made it into the hearts and minds of children while they were still young. By the time he took the children back to the resort for lunch, he had already formed some ideas on how to start and proceed toward this new goal.

Nagnag: You've done this work for a long time with adults. You have been successful at it, so far, but that doesn't mean you can be as successful with children. Doing it for your own kids and grandkids is different from doing it with others' kids. What makes you believe you can?

Maximus: Because I know I can. Except this time it will be more of a collective effort.

Nagnag: What makes you sure that he would be on board?

Maximus: I know he wants the best for his children and that he can relate to them. I also know that he is my son, which increases the chance that he will see the value where I see it.

Nagnag: I think your intentions are great, but I'm not sure about the outcome. Besides, you're on vacation. Can't you just do this after you rest? You have plenty of time when you get back.

Maximus: You do a good job of living up to your name, Nagnag. While I feel you may be right and I deserve a break, I have learned over time that you don't necessarily look out for my best interests.

Nagnag: You doubt my intentions again.

Maximus: You taught me to do so, my pain in the neck, mandated life partner.

Nagnag: Time will tell. I know you can act on it right away and I know I won't be waiting for long. So we'll see, Mr. Dream Big.

Maximus: I just love it when you call me that and I like it even more when you challenge me. You have made me more determined to make it happen. You're right, time will tell and it won't be a long time.

It was early evening when Maximus called his son, Maher, to join him in his room.

Maher: Hey Dad, is everything all right?

Maximus: I wanted to share a couple of thoughts with you and get your opinion.

Maher: Of course.

Maximus: Well, I had an interesting experience this morning with Farris. He was talking about swimming without his life vest, not because of any specific reason except that he did not want to be embarrassed. Of course, I wanted to understand where he got that thought, and he shared with me that it was from TV and his parents. Now I am sure that Farris is not the only child at his age, or maybe a little older, who experiences these kinds of thoughts and feelings. I want to make sure that we do our part to ensure that children grow up free of destructive thoughts and emotions that will prevent them from living their lives fully.

What dawned on me is that I have been doing this work with adults for many years and I was hoping that they would share that knowledge as it impacts their lives. But as you know, we all get busy and wrapped up in many things. I believe that children will take their course in life. However, we tend to forget that part of the course may cost them many years of their lives. So I was thinking about what we can do to influence the lives of the children as far as we can reach. What do you think?

Maher: Dad, this is not news to me. You have spent your life creating ways and systems to improve the lives of whoever comes your way. You have always made a positive influence on people and I have no doubt that you will do the same this time. I believe in my heart that it will be a phenomenal experience for today's children and for the ones to come. So, what do you have in mind?

Maximus: Children learn mostly from their parents. Also children learn best when they play. So I am trying to think of a way that can combine both parental input and play to create the most impact on their lives. Can you imagine a generation of children afraid of nothing? A generation who believes that everything is possible? A generation that does not have disabling words as part of their vocabulary? Words like "can't," "impossible," "don't know," "have no choice" and the like. A generation that knows no limit to dreams, no boundaries to achievements, and no end to human ability. A generation that stays young until the last breath of their lives. Imagine how amazing that generation could be and how promising for the generations that followed?

Maher: That sounds phenomenal, Dad. I would love nothing more for my children than to be free of all the obstacles that limit their potential and make the world a better place for themselves and for others who will come after them. I am on board, what do you have in mind?

Maximus: I thought we would start with a pilot program. We'll try this in-house. The effort will be focused on the parents and the children. It is my duty to ensure that parents understand their roles and are equipped with the proper tools to go on and be successful in this pilot program. And it is your duty to equip the children with the right tools and the proper understanding of how to overcome the hindering thoughts and emotions of failure and fear.

Maher: Dad, this is a big responsibility. I will need your help. Remember, I am a father myself so I will need to be trained among the rest of the parents in our family.

Maximus: I realize that, son, and I realize that you will have a quantum role in this effort. Therefore, we will go with the parents' education and training first so you can have your portion of it and you can benefit from it before beginning your duties. I wanted to share the plan with you today so we could discuss the details and build the structure to achieve our goal. I don't want you to be concerned about how big the effort is, as it will drive itself to success. As long as we believe, it will work for the best of all concerned.

Maher: I am not concerned about that. I trust your planning and I am all the way behind you, as I have always been. I am listening. Bring it on.

Maximus: I will propose the idea to the parents in our family tonight around the dinner table so that we can sense their preparation and buy-in and also give them the opportunity to be part of the plan. And I hope they will share with us how much time they can dedicate to this effort. We must not forget that they are on vacation and I don't want them to think I set them up so I can train them. What do you think?

Maher: I think it's a great approach. Now what do you have in mind for my part? I am getting anxious.

Maximus: You, my son, the proclaimed play writer... are going to write a play for the children. The children of our family will be the actors in the play and they will perform it in the next few days before going home. That way the children will have a chance to live their roles, understand their concepts, engrave the memory in their minds and hearts, and make their parents proud as they teach them what they learned and what they expect from that day on.

Maher: This is extraordinary, Dad. This is phenomenal. This is brilliant. And I don't think it will take me long to come up with a play, since it needs to be long enough to convey the message but short enough to maintain everyone's focus. I'm thinking of a 10-minute play. What do you think?

Maximus: I think this is perfect.

Maher: And I see a challenge already. How am I going to translate the concepts that you have been teaching adults so that those concepts can be easily understood and grasped by the mind of a child?

Maximus: I am glad you asked that question, son. I have not figured that out and I was hoping that, being the genius of playwriting you are, you would make it all possible. One more factor we cannot ignore is how intelligent the children are. We often tend to think of them as less intelligent than they actually are. I have not met a child yet who is not smarter than most adults and more receptive than any sponge I have come across.

Maher: I am not going to hide my anxiety but I have faith that this will be brilliant. It is brilliant.

Maximus: Excellent. I had no doubt you would be on board. I had no doubt that your good nature would position you exactly where you need to be to impact the world. All right, be prepared for the discussion around the dinner table. It will be fun.

Maher: Dad, one more thing. How can we bring our idea up during dinnertime so that it is acceptable to both the parents and the children?

Maximus: We will not go into the details. We will suggest it as a pilot program that the family will have the privilege of trying before it goes anywhere else. The success of the participants in the pilot program will dictate its feasibility to live and thrive in the outside world while it remains as a fun family activity. What do you think?

Maher: I'm glad you have the answer, Dad, because it would've taken me some time to think about it. I'm ready and I will be waiting for dinner.

It was dinnertime, and Elektra rang her bell as usual for everybody to come out and take their seats around the table. A couple of hours later, as everyone ate and talked, Maximus asked his family a question and offered a special present to the one who had the right answer.

"Who can tell me who is human's best friend and who is the worst enemy?"

"Carmen, the monarch butterfly, is my best friend and I have no enemies, Grandpa," said Karam as she jumped out of her chair.

"That is a very good try, my princess. I am looking for a different answer. Let me be more specific. I see all of your faces with big question marks, so let me help. Your best friend is the one who helps you do anything and everything you want. Your worst enemy is the one who stops you from doing anything and everything you want. Who are they?"

Everyone came up with a different answer but not what Maximus was looking for. "What would you do if I told you about a secret recipe that will make you so powerful in life? A recipe that empowers you to achieve anything you hope for and have everything you want?"

"I am in, Grandpa," said Aidan, as Maximus had expected. The other children followed, as they always followed his lead.

"You are giving us the secret and you're giving us a present?" asked Leila.

"The secret is a present," said Maximus.

"It must be a very powerful secret. I am in, Dad" said Leila as she raised her right hand for everyone to join the fun and the joyful spirit. All raised their hands as well and chanted "I am in."

"This is great, so here's the deal," explained Maximus. "I will need from the parents one hour a day for the next three days. This will be part of a pilot program that we will have the chance to experience and enjoy. Depending on how well we do, we may introduce this program to others so they can benefit as well. And you may have the pleasure of building a program that will impact mankind in the future. How does that sound?"

"I am still in, Dad," said Maher as he raised his hand. The rest of the parents raised their hands and said in scattered voices, "Sure thing" "Why not?" and "We are still in."

"Outstanding. Then we will start tomorrow an hour before sunset and we can do it on the beach so we can enjoy watching the sun afterwards. How does that sound?"

"Good planning, honey. You have always been good at that," said Elektra as she stood up to bring sweets for the family to enjoy.

The next day, Maximus headed to the shore. He made it to the shore before anyone else did as he was truly committed to his goal. A few minutes later, the whole group arrived and got themselves together in a circle as Maximus joined them to sit on the sandy beach. He asked, "Who among you has failed the most so far?"

It took a few minutes and some courage for one among them to speak up and say, "That would be me, Dad. I flunked more classes in high school than any one of my siblings," said Maher.

"You missed the scale to measure failure, then. I think that would be me," interrupted Allen, Leila's husband.

"What made you say that, son?" asked Maximus.

"As you know, from the first time I came to you asking for your blessing and permission to marry your daughter, that I failed in building my business 16 times."

"Sixteen times? I thought it was only three times," said Leila.

"That's true, honey. It was three times after I met you and 13 times before that. So you can see what a lucky charm you are to me."

Maximus asked, "What made you hold on to it?"

Allen: The first few times it was stubbornness. After that it was something else. At first I did not like the taste of defeat and I wanted to prove to myself that I could do it. The first few times, I failed miserably. I had no clue what I was doing or why I was defeated. About the seventh time, I learned how to avoid some mistakes and I changed my strategy a little bit. I still failed but without making the same mistakes. So I learned that if I paid attention to certain things and tried something else that the results would tell me what was wrong. There was no guarantee. There was a lot of trial and error but I still made progress every single time I tried.

Maximus: How do you describe your feelings when you were failing?

Allen: It was terrible. In the beginning, it was a pure challenge to prove to myself what I could and could not do. But then it became more about how I could make things better and succeed. So I guess in the beginning I was focusing more on myself but as I continued failing, I became more and more focused on the business and its success than myself.

Maximus: Tell me more.

Allen: I think that in the beginning I focused more on making sure not to fail. And the more I focused on not failing, the more I failed. You might say that I surrounded myself with the feelings of failure and my attempts to avoid it. Later, I did not care about failing as much as understanding more of what I had done wrong and what I could do better. I would say that failure in the beginning was a concern of mine. Once I focused more on the business, I shifted my attention toward success and I completely forgot about failure. On my 12th try, I actually did not mind failing because I found failure to be helpful. It was thanks to failure that I learned what I had done wrong and what I could do better.

Maximus: That's a lot of bravery and honesty. Nicely put, son. I heard you saying that failure prepared you. How's that?

Allen: Failure taught me what I was doing wrong, how often I did it and how I did it. It was a simple way of teaching me what would not work.

Maximus: If you were teaching Karam one lesson about failure, and it would be the only lesson you could teach her and she would use it for the rest of her life, what would it be?

Allen: I would share with her one of the highlights from one of your workshops: *"Befriend failure for it is your best partner in reaching success."* I would teach her that failure is not here to scare her; instead it is here to teach her and show her the way to success. The more you fail, the more you learn, and the closer you get to success.

Maximus: How embarrassed were you every time you failed?

Allen: The first few times I could not even look at myself in the mirror, that's how embarrassed I was. Later, I shared my failures with my close friends. I told them why I had failed and how silly it was to make those mistakes. It was actually empowering to share with them the mistakes I had made and the lessons I had learned. They were not failures to me at that point as much as they were lessons. I was proud to advertise to my friends that I knew what they didn't know. Failure was embarrassing to me at first but it was a source of empowerment and self-confidence later.

Maximus: You saved me the time of asking the next question. So, what you're saying is that embarrassment will be there as long as we think of failure as mere failure. However, if we thought of failure as a teacher, that would empower us and raise our confidence, allowing us to teach others. How accurate is that?

Allen: That's exactly what I meant, Uncle.

Maximus: How would you teach Karam that principle?

Allen: I'm not sure I can teach her that but I am sure she will learn it on her own as she learns that failure is her best friend.

Maximus: Thank you, Allen. I have always admired your perseverance, wisdom and the way you take care of my daughter.

Maximus asked the others, "What do you think?"

"I think the concept is great and putting it to work will be very challenging," said Leila, who received nods from the others, agreeing with her comment.

Maximus: Where do you see the challenge, daughter?

Leila: It is difficult to tell somebody to go ahead and fail. And it can be hard to believe, deep inside, that failure is okay.

Maximus: Where do you believe the concern is? Is it in the other person or in you?

Leila: I think I would start with myself. I agree with the concept, but in practice I don't like to fail and that leads me to not try because I don't like the feeling of failure.

Maximus: You stop yourself from pursuing something just because you are afraid to fail. How accurate is that?

Leila: That is quite accurate.

Maximus: You have been a great help, my daughter. Fear is our topic for tomorrow. I kept you long enough for today and I don't want to keep you longer from having fun on your vacation. And I would never stand between you and this memorable sunset.

Maximus waved his arm, as if to introduce the people gathered to the sunset behind him. Then, he took a walk on the beach, his head full of plans, assessing what he was going to do next to ensure the small group of parents were 100% prepared to nourish their kids to have healthy lives.

The next day, around the same time, Maximus headed to the beach to meet with the group again. As he made it to the shore he found everybody in a circle waiting for him. He realized how committed they were to the process. As he approached the group, he heard them talking about the subject that had been discussed the day before.

"Allen, I am trying to understand how to become friends with failure while fear is overtaking me," said Leila.

"Well, the interesting thing is that I have seen it happen before my eyes," said Muheeb. "My son Aidan is a perfect example of befriending failure. I remember him, as an infant, grabbing what he wanted without even thinking twice about it. I also remember he started doing that before he was able to walk. He would get up to walk a couple of feet, or maybe even a foot and a half, and then fall. Every time he fell, he just got up and tried to walk again. Even the times when he was hurt, he would cry and get up and continue walking. At the time I thought this boy must be glutton for punishment or just stubborn like his dad. However, I realized later that, naturally, that's how we all are.

"When we are new in this life we go by our nature. Our nature is to go for whatever it is we would like to have. Our nature does not know fear of trying or pursuing. Fear comes along later as we experience life. Or we condition ourselves to think about what we can do and cannot do and we start doubting ourselves. I remember that Aidan, when he was about four years old, wanted to learn how to walk on our thin fence by keeping his balance. He tried that many times, and he fell many times, and he didn't succeed until he broke a couple of fingers. While I was not happy with what he got himself into, later when I thought about it, I actually admired his persistence."

"Would you call that persistence or stubbornness?" asked Leila.

"I believe there is a thin line between stubbornness and persistence. Maybe our dad can tell us about it," said Maher.

"What do you think, son? What is the difference between stubbornness and persistence?"

"My understanding, Dad, is that persistence is not very different from stubbornness. I am not sure if I can tell the difference between the two."

"How about you, Leila? You asked the question, what do you think?"

"Well, Dad, I think for the most part it is stubbornness because if you see yourself or somebody else getting hurt, and you keep doing what you have been doing then that is not smart. And if it's not smart then it is stubbornness."

Maximus thought about it for a moment and said, "What I think you're saying is that persistence is related to studying the risk and its outcome and what could be done better so you can achieve your goal. Stubbornness, on the other hand, is not studying the risk and actually ignoring the same mistakes over and over again without improving anything."

Leila replied, "That's pretty much it, Dad. I think you hit the nail on the head. I think it's all about risk."

"Tell me more. What do you mean it is all about risk?"

"Well, I believe we feel fear because we are not willing to take risks."

"What I hear you saying is that risk is the source of fear. So what is risk?"

"I'm not sure, Dad. I think it's anything that is not worth pursuing. Well, I take that back because we wouldn't know ahead of time what is worth pursuing or not unless we knew the future."

"Very interesting. I like how you came back and looked at it from a different perspective. What you said is that we determine the value of anything that we are going to pursue and that value will make us take that risk or not take it."

"That's correct, Dad. However it is all in the future and there's no way to be concrete."

"You just defined what risk is, daughter. Risk, as you just stated, is something of the future, or some event in the future. If we knew the future, we would know what we must do now. However, because it is in the future and it is unknown, it is a risk. By nature, mankind doesn't like the unknown. Okay, great. So we agree that risk is whatever we consider unknown. Now, let's go back to fear. What is fear?"

"Well, I can tell you the scientific definition of what fear is and where it comes from, however, I don't think that would be quite helpful to us right now. So let me see how I can do that in simple terms," said Maher.

"That would be wonderful, brother," said Leila and everyone laughed.

"Okay, fear is a state of mind, however, we refer to it as a very uncomfortable feeling. If we talk about risk, for example, then we are referring to fear of the unknown. And if we are concerned about the unknown, the thoughts are translated to an uncomfortable feeling, possibly anxiety, about what may happen to us if that undesirable event takes place. That is fear in simple terms."

"Is fear a thought or a feeling?" asked Maximus.

"Dad, as you know every feeling starts with a thought, so I would say that fear is a thought initially and we know it as a feeling," said Maher.

"Tell me more, son. I want to know more about that."

"Well, when we think of a risk, an unknown event that may happen in the future, we may think of what is undesirable about that event. So we are still talking about thoughts. Those thoughts stimulate the mind to imagine and see the state that we don't like. That is fear. However, when we think about that undesirable event and we see that image, we immediately respond to it with a feeling, without realizing that we actually thought about it first."

"I can go with that. I buy it. What about you guys?"

When Maximus looked around he saw everybody nodding in agreement. He felt that everyone was comfortable with the concepts of fear and risk. "To summarize what you are saying, fear is driven by the thought of taking a risk. The risk is an event that takes place in the future and its outcome is unknown. As a result, the thoughts of the outcome, from the unknown event, drive other thoughts of discomfort called 'fear.' Fear would translate to an uncomfortable feeling, such as one that is described as 'butterflies in the stomach.' Good so far?"

"I think we're good with that, Dad," said Leila.

"Now my question to you is how do you overcome fear?"

Maximus waited for an answer as everyone looked around at each other.

"This scenario by itself could be an example of fear," said Maximus.

"What do you mean, Dad?" asked Leila.

"How likely is it that no one wanted to answer because they might give the wrong answer or be embarrassed?"

"That's a good possibility," said Leila as she smiled.

"What went through your head after I asked that question?" Maximus asked.

Leila answered, "What immediately came to my mind were a couple of possible answers. However, I didn't know which one would be the right answer and I didn't know if they would make sense to everybody. So, I thought it would be better to wait and see if anyone else would say anything to either validate or negate what I had in mind. If they validated my thought, then I would know that I had the answer. If they negated it, or gave a different answer, I would learn something new and save myself the embarrassment."

"There you go again. That fear of embarrassment. What is the big deal about fear of embarrassment? I keep hearing about it over and over again. Can anyone help me?"

"Well, Dad, it's probably more of a female thing and probably something you cannot relate to. What do you guys think?" asked Leila.

"No, honey, I don't think it's a female thing, I think we can all relate," Allen said.

"Talk about yourself my friend. How do you know guys feel the same way females do?" asked Maher as he laughed. And he made everyone else laugh with him. Then he resumed, "I agree with you. I was just joking. Fear does not care about a male or female. Fear is in all of us and the worry of being embarrassed is in all of us. I agree that it has different levels from one person to another; nevertheless, it exists in every one of us."

"Well, I think we worry about being embarrassed because we worry too much about what others may think of us," said Maher.

"I agree with you, son. Think back to the early years of your life, and if you cannot, think of your kids. When did the change happen? When did you, if you remember, or your kids, start worrying about what others may think?"

"I'm thinking about Aidan again, since he is my firstborn and I have learned a lot from him. I don't think he started worrying about what others thought until he started school. Before then, he did whatever he thought was right to do. He didn't worry about what Mom and Dad would think about him doing this or that. He just did it. Somehow over time, and as he entered school, he learned that certain things he did required validation or acceptance. I believe that's when his behavior changed and the fear started showing up." said Muheeb.

"A wise man once said that when you're 18 you care about what others think of you. When you're in your 40s, you don't care about what anybody else thinks of you. And when you're in your 60s you learn that no one else really cared about you at all," said Maximus.

"The more I think about it, the more I realize that people don't care about anything but validating themselves, so I should not worry about them validating or not validating my views," said Allen.

"I think we agree that most of our concerns about being embarrassed are fears of other people's opinions of us—more than our opinion of ourselves," said Maximus.

"That is very true," said Leila, "If I didn't worry about what others thought of what I wore, what I said, or what I did, then I would just do it all. And if I failed, if I didn't like the results, then I would simply make different choices, because no one would judge me for it."

Maximus nodded. "Very interesting. You mentioned a very good word: judging. What you're saying is you are afraid of judgment. How accurate is that?"

"I think that is very accurate," said Leila.

"Let me ask you all one more thing. Let's assume that you lived in a town by yourself where everything was available to you. And you had all these things in mind that you wanted to achieve. You wanted to write a book for yourself, create a play for yourself, build a new program for yourself, build an artistic building the way you envisioned, and do all kinds of things in many different areas of your life. But they were just for you. How likely is it that you would fear failure?"

"You wouldn't feel fear because the only standards would be yours," said Allen.

"Perfect. It seems that we judge ourselves against certain standards that mankind created, regardless of good or bad, so we can achieve them. Or overcome them. Once we achieve our goals, we qualify that as a success. If we don't achieve them, then we would classify that as a failure. How true is that?"

"I would say, from my own experience, that is very true," said Allen.

"The question becomes how do we get ourselves as close as possible to the standards so that we don't fear failure?" asked

Maximus. That was a tough question for everyone and it took them a few minutes to think about it.

Allen was the most experienced with failure, so he came back with what he thought was the right answer. "Well, I think even the standards themselves change every day and depend on the group of people that we are addressing. However, the more we try to accomplish something, the closer we get to the acceptable standards—the universe's standards. We don't know the exact recipe for success when we start but we know how to try, and by trying we can learn the right approach."

"That is a very good way of looking at it, son. What you're saying is that failure and fear are connected and they cannot be separated. Does that resonate with you all?" After a few seconds Maximus saw heads nodding in agreement.

Maher said, "After all, if we were not concerned about failing we would not feel fear. Of course we're not talking about fear of death, or fear of a hungry saber tooth tiger running behind us, because those days are gone. Rather, I am talking about today's type of fear—the fear that is based on our worries about our ability to achieve, be validated, and be accepted. Of course facing a train running at full speed will inspire a very natural fear that is normal but I don't believe this is what we are addressing. Is that right?"

"That is correct, son. And that's what I would like to make sure that we are capturing today before the sunset comes upon us. So let me ask the question one more time. How do you overcome fear? Take your time to think about it. Your answer is very important for what is coming up," said Maximus, as he leaned back with his hands against the sand.

Maher leaned forward, indicating that he believed his answer was ready and said, "I think the best way to beat fear is to fail, and fail as many times as possible. I believe, like Allen shared with us yesterday, that the more you fail, the more you learn. The more you learn, the wiser you become. When you know what you're supposed to do versus what you're not supposed to do, your self-confidence grows and, as a result, fear diminishes over time."

"Nicely said, son. Who else?"

"I agree with Maher," said Allen. "I've failed many times. Each time I learned something new and I came back with a correction to the actions that I had taken. Every time I corrected my actions, and the correction worked favorably, I boosted my self-confidence, and I felt less fear. My relationship with fear became more of an understanding one. I know fear exists and is not going anywhere. And fear knows that I am persistent and I am going to continue toward my goal no matter how many times I fail.

"I will leave it at that. I don't think I can say it better," said Maximus. He looked around and he was very pleased with the day's session. He realized that the parents in his family were better prepared at this point. He knew that, with a little bit more work, they could control their emotions about fear and failure. He was confident that they were on a roll and would make a difference in their children's lives and the lives of generations to come.

He sat down to enjoy the sunset with his family.

The next day, Maximus headed to the shore to meet with the parents, like he had done the previous two days. He wanted to make sure everyone was ready before the kids' training started. When he arrived, he found the parents talking about the fun activities they had enjoyed during the day. "Hello, family. How's everything going?" Everyone answered with happiness and contentment.

Maximus thought for a few seconds and then he said, "Allen, I've always admired your story about how you started your own business. I don't know how many of us know the details. How do you feel about telling us the juicy details?"

"It was interesting but I don't want to bore you with something that I have already shared," said Allen.

"Well, what I would like for you to share with us today is how you *lived* your experience. What are the moments that live in your memory? That's what you will probably share only with your kids and your grandkids. So I think maybe I am being a little greedy and I'm asking for too much. I am hoping that we can enjoy the experience that your kids and grandkids will enjoy in the future. How will that work for you?"

"That would be my pleasure." Allen crossed his legs as he sat down and grabbed a little stick and started drawing lines in the sand. He looked around and said, "I had an unstoppable desire and unlimited passion about printing. I remember, when I was 19, I was introduced to 'Aldus Pius Manutius.' Mr. Manutius was an Italian humanist who was a printer and publisher and he founded the Aldine class at Venice. He also invented the italic type. I was intrigued by his determination and his love for printing and publishing. And I found myself, over time, buried in books to the point that I enjoyed the ink smell on paper more than my own cologne. I had this idea in my mind that I could start a majestic and glorious printing house that did what the printing houses used to do. This printing house of mine would use the old method of printing, which would add authenticity to the books and preserve the old books' style before it vanished.

"I wanted to have something completely different. I wanted to build something that was part of the industry yet considered 'out of the box.' I wanted all the books and publications that came to my print house to be taken in a specific order and have a unique design. I imagined the publishing house would have a fine reputation and a large clientele and people would race to buy our products as soon as they heard the name of the print house.

"My passion drove me beyond my ability and my knowledge of the industry. There was so much I didn't know about printing, about business, and about the market. But I had a picture in my mind that I thought about all the time. It was a picture I saw in one of the museums—a woodblock form from 1568—of two printers, handcrafting books.

I resisted all financial help from my family. I wanted to make it my own experience. I wanted to start my printing house with whatever I had in my pockets—not only to make it happen, but also to make it a success. I had my own definition of success. I believed I would be successful if I started from scratch and made it to the top by relying entirely on my own thinking and my financial ability. Today, when I think about that time, I realize there were things that I did not understand. I had no idea what rotary printing was, or intaglio, offset press, screen-printing, flexography... I didn't know any details about any of these things except their names and what I had read. But that didn't stop me!

"My first adventure was to look for an old printing press machine that printed in the same way as in the days of Mr. Manutius. I spent a few months doing research and I eventually landed on a good ad. I contacted the owner to buy it from him. When I visited the owner, and I told him about my plan, he laughed at me and he said this machine was fit only for a museum. He said he thought that I was representing a museum. He insisted that the machine would not work, however, my passion blinded me and I said that I still wanted to buy it and I would try to make it work.

"I was ecstatic just looking at the machine every single morning when I woke up. But I had spent every penny I had on buying that machine. That was my first mistake and evidence of my lack of knowledge. I spent about six months after that trying to learn how to work the machine and not learning very much. Six more months passed and I still had not made a dime.

"I started feeling the pressure—and the embarrassment. That's when everyone around me began commenting, making fun of my approach. I heard it all: I didn't know what I was doing, I was a dreamer, I was living in the wrong time, I wanted to bring back the past, I had no clue what business is about, I was an intruder to the industry and I was over my head. I heard it all, on and on. I felt so embarrassed that I started to hear the words in my mind.

"Yet my passion and my belief that I could make it happen kept me going. I started reading publications about how to succeed in the printing business. I learned some things from my research and was emboldened and I felt prepared to apply them immediately. I had no money, but I had to find a way. I did find some financing but six months later I failed again and then I owed money to the bank. I had never owed money in my life. At that point I began to feel fear—the fear of failure and the judgment that comes with it. While I realized that I was embarrassed, I was more fearful. I was afraid that I would need to ask my family for help after initially rejecting their support.

"I didn't know anything about business strategy, marketing, planning, how to hire employees or manage them; I had no knowledge of anything that I needed to know to start a successful business. So, I took classes at a community college to understand basics of business and entrepreneurship. As I learned basic strategies, I applied them to my business immediately. I had to ask for a couple more loans from the bank to support myself through school and through the beginning stages of building my business.

"You may wonder by now what kept me going as I failed so many times. Well, I slowly started to see some progress. As funny as it may sound, I found myself failing less. I started to see failure coming my way before it happened. I kept moving to see exactly where failure would show up. I knew that I was failing but I also knew I was learning. My learning was so robust that whenever I made a mistake, I would follow up with a new course of action toward the same target. The new course of action would sometimes fail, but it did not fail in exactly the same way it had the first time.

"It took five years to get on my feet. By the sixth year, I was able to cover my debt—all of it—with a little left over. That was my confirmation that I was on the right path. I knew, deep in my heart, that there was no substitute for taking action. I then took action all the time. Although I knew that failure was waiting for me on the other side, I still took action, because I knew that I would learn something from it."

Allen stopped talking and he looked around; it seemed everyone was waiting for what would come next.

Maximus spoke up, "I have always enjoyed the way you talk about your business and how you established it. No matter what you came up against, you always knew the importance of taking action. I heard something today that I had not heard before. I heard you saying that you knew failure was on the other side and you took action anyway. Then you went back and checked the plan see what was wrong so you could improve it."

Allen: Indeed. Going back to assess the results was definitely one of the best things I learned over time. It helped me understand what failed, how it failed and why it failed. Assessing the end result was necessary to see the new possibilities that the next action might bring, thus it empowered me to face failure again.

Maximus: So what you're saying is taking action alone is not enough. Reassessing is essential. How accurate is that?

Allen: Absolutely!

Maximus: Great. In your story you illustrated everything we have talked about so far. You talked about failure, fear, taking action and reassessing for better planning. If you were to put those concepts together for the youth of the world, so they could learn something early in life, carry on your advice for the rest of their lives, and be equipped with better tools for the future, how would you go about that? How would you say it in one crisp sentence?

Allen: Embrace your fear of failure, reassess failure and take action anyway for action takers are the winners of the world.

"Beautifully put, son," said Maximus. "I think Allen summarized it all beautifully for us. And this is the first part of our journey," said Maximus as he stood up and shook the sand from his hands. He helped the others to get up so they could move closer to the water and enjoy the sunset one more time as students of life.

Elektra rang the bell for dinnertime. Everyone who heard it came running because they were racing to fill their bellies with Grandma's tasty food. Maher still had not shown up, even after everyone had gathered around the table. Elektra questioned his absence and Maher's wife said he was in his room, busy writing something and he did not want to be disturbed. Maximus suggested that everyone proceeds with dinner and he would go and check on Maher.

Maximus: Hey, son. You're not coming to join us for dinner?

Maher: Oh, Dad, I just had so much in my head that I wanted to put it all on paper.

Maximus looked around and he saw paper all over the place.

Maximus: You have been busy, haven't you?

Maher: I just keep writing my thoughts, and I have others that are racing to hit the paper but I can't organize them.

Maximus: Well, I suggest you give it a break. Perhaps eating dinner with your family will inspire you and give you tranquility that will settle your thoughts. What do you think?

Maher: I don't want to give up on this now.

Maximus: I don't think that by joining us for dinner you will be giving up on what you have in your mind. You are only taking a breather to sort out your thoughts and have an easier time organizing them. What do you say?

Maher: I can try that, but I will need to come back soon after dinner to finish this. Based on what I have in my head, I may need the next day or two to get the children ready. What kind of plan do you have for this, Dad?

Maximus: I will leave that up to you. You tell me what you want to do. I believe my job so far is done and the rest of the planning is yours.

Maher: That's a lot of pressure on me, but I am thankful for your confidence in me. I won't let you down. It will be great.

Maximus: Oh, son. I have never doubted you. Let's go, they're waiting. I can smell the food all the way from here. I don't know how you can write when the food smells this good.

Maher ate quickly then said, "Excuse me, I have something in my mind that I need to put on paper and I know that you will support me. It won't be long. I will be back soon." It was about an hour later when Maher gathered the children in his room and started talking to them about the play.

"Aidan, Farris, Aban, Karam, I have a phenomenal experience for you. I know you all like to read and you all like plays. What do you think about us staging a play for the family?"

"That is awesome, Uncle. I love it. What is my role in the play?" asked Karam.

"That is great, Dad. That sounds really good," Farris said.

Maher explained to the children, "We'll perform a play about the thoughts and emotions that keep people from becoming successful and being winners in life."

"Do you mean like the things Grandpa teaches ?" asked Aidan.

"That's exactly it. What do you all think?" They all nodded and they jumped out of their places, excited to do something that was connected to what their grandfather does. They always loved to hear his stories and they always heard everybody talking about what a sophisticated and good teacher he is. But still, they never knew exactly what his teaching was about. Maher spent the next hour reading to the kids their roles and telling them about the background of the play. He repeated this over and over again so they could grasp the ideas. "Okay, kids, it is time to get some rest because we have a lot of work to do tomorrow. You now have an idea about our project. Tomorrow is a big day for practice and hopefully we will be done by dinnertime. Do you have any thoughts?"

They all jumped out of their seats. "Uncle, I can't go to sleep now. I have to memorize my role," said Karam.

"She is right, Uncle. I don't think I will be able to sleep, either. I'm so excited, I want to do the play now," said Aidan.

"Come on, Dad. We are still awake and would love to spend more time together. And this is a really cool thing to spend time doing. Let's do it now," said Farris.

"Well, we can do a little bit of it but we need to get to sleep so that we will have enough energy for tomorrow. So let's practice for another half hour, and then we need to go to bed. How does that sound?"

The children jumped up and down in excitement. Maher said, "Now I will hand each of you your part in the play. It is not very long. Read it as many times as you can and let me know if there's a word that is difficult for you or that is new to you and we will work it out together. How's that?"

They snatched the papers from Maher's hand and started reading. If you had been standing about a hundred feet away you would have heard something like the buzzing of an extremely active beehive. The children were saying their lines over and over again, repeating the words with emotion, as if they were actors of many years. Maher was confident that he did not need to do anything more at this point and it would be great if he just stepped out of their way. He left them in the room and went to see his father. "Dad, I think it is going to be amazing. The kids are already in 100%. They are memorizing their roles now as they couldn't even wait until tomorrow."

"They are my grandchildren. You should know better," said Maximus as he smiled and grabbed Maher to hug him.

Before the kids went to bed, Maher made a request. "There's a very important piece of information you need to know. In order to make this play successful, you can talk to no one about it. You can practice in front of no one. This is our group, and we need to keep it as a secret between us until we perform it. What do you say?" They nodded in agreement. They spent the next day practicing at the beach. They stayed a distance from their parents. Their parents could see them doing something but they had no idea what it was. It was heartening to see their children fully engaged, committed and focused. At night, and before dinner, Maher asked the kids to come to his room to check on their memorization.

"How's it going?"

"We are ready, Uncle" said Aidan.

"Great! How about you practice it for me?"

"Absolutely," said Aidan.

The first rehearsal of the play was encouraging; the kids had already memorized their parts.

"This is phenomenal. We will take a rest tonight and we will do two or three rehearsals tomorrow during the day so that we can show the family what we have after dinner as they are enjoying their dessert. How does that sound?"

The kids jumped up and down as if they could not wait but Maher assured them it would be worth it. The next day dragged on a little long for the kids. They gathered in different places to practice a few more times. Maher was ecstatic about what he saw. It was finally dinnertime. More than 80 people joined the wide circle of tables that Elektra set up for this dinner. The children sat together, as they normally did, but they did not eat much. They looked at Maher and gestured to ask about the time. During dinner Maher announced to the family, "Family and friends. I hope you are planning to stay with us for the rest of the evening, as we normally do, to enjoy dessert. Tonight we have a special treat. 'The Phenomenal Four' are here to show us a play that I am sure you will find inspiring."

As dessert was served, Maher and the kids gathered in the middle of the dinner area, where they were properly positioned to start the play. Maher was the narrator. He had a little drum in his left hand and a small stick in his right hand. He hit the drum nine times in a fast pace, then hit it once more... then once again... then for the last time. Everyone was quiet and shifted their attention toward him. He said, "Karam was a four-year-old girl who lived in a very small town and spent most of her time with her beautiful family. One day, Karam heard her older brother talking about success. He said that there is nothing that can match the feeling of success. He said that success was the ultimate place to be. She heard him say that this beautiful place, called success, is the dreamers' island where only special people live. She also heard him say that the 'Success Express' train is the only way for anyone to make it to Success Island. He said that the train would depart from anywhere as long as the person was ready to board, even if it was next to their barn. Karam wanted to experience that feeling and she wanted to go to Success Island.

"The next morning she woke up early, as usual. She went to the barn and had a conversation with her horse, like she did every day. Karam asked her horse if he knew anything about Success Island and if the 'Success Express' train had passed by today. The horse whinnied and said 'I have been to Success Island many times. The 'Success Express' will come when we are ready to board. If you are ready, then go to the side of the barn.'

"Karam started walking toward the side of the barn as her horse had instructed. As she stepped through the giant barn door, she saw a big pile that she hadn't noticed before. She went close to it to find out more. As she got closer, she noticed that the pile was moving, so she asked..."

(Karam steps in the middle of the stage and says): "Who are you and what are you doing here?"

"I am fear.

I am always near.

To your heart I will never be dear.

So when you see me, out of my way you must steer," said Farris.

"Dear Fear,

I never knew much about you in my life's first year.

I have learned, so far, that you are a pain in the rear.

So why are you here?"

"I live in the minds of the weak, my dear.

I make sure they are never clear.

And they are always stuck in a stinky mere."

"You are a distraction as I hear.

And you are stronger in the minds that allow you to appear.

I have long decided to cheer.

That way I see my path clear.

And control my mind's gear.

I will always overcome your frontier.

I will always make my life an eventful premier.

And in a front of resistance, you can only disappear.

What do you have to say now, Mr. Fear?"

"You are right, my dear,

In front of your resistance I can only disappear," said Farris, as he crumbled down to become a tiny pile that could barely be noticed.

Karam went along until she saw another pile. She got closer to it and she asked, "And who are you?"

"I am Failure the slaver.

I come in any kind and flavor.

I lead you to embarrassment, lack of confidence, and any bad feeling or behavior.

I chase you, as long as you let me, like a hungry alligator.

If nothing comes to mind, think of me as your jailer," said Aban.

"Dear Failure the slaver,

I also hear that you can be a saver.

You can destroy, you can help, and you can be a warrior.

You can make the days unclear and even grayer.

How about a deal, my dear Failure?

We become partners and you will be my savior?"

"You seem to be quite optimistic.

Fear and I are disempowering and ballistic.

However; you seem to be quite mystic, or maybe beyond simplistic.

Are you suggesting I become friendly and artistic?"

"I have heard that you can even be a phenomenal teacher.

And beyond a magnificent help and creature.

What do I need to learn from your unique feature?"

"My dear, your confidence is bountiful.

I live only in a soul that is doubtful.

To that soul I, along with fear, am quite harmful.

You, on the other hand, are hopeful.

I can advise you with what you will forever find useful.

Always, to yourself, be truthful.

Against Fear and Failure be forceful.

Devour Action until you are super full.

I am honored to be your teacher as long as you are masterful."

"I knew you would be helpful.

You are immensely wonderful.

Thank you for teaching me to be powerful.

I will make life colorful and help every soul become delightful."

"As soon as she finished her sentence she heard,

Do I hear my name? Was I mentioned as admirable or vain?" said Aidan.

"You must be Action, my dear. You were certainly mentioned for gain.

I believe you are the last link of the chain."

"I am the best of the chain.

Losers may think of me as unnecessarily vain.

However I am to procrastinators a sharp vane.

I bring winners their destiny faster than a bullet train.

I keep achievers always in the success lane.

And if you procrastinate I will forever abstain.

So, my dear, who are you and what do you want to attain?"

"I am a winner hoping that you explain

How can I board your train?

I am as thirsty for success as the ground is thirsty for rain.

I hear that your results drive people insane.

Please, teach me how not to refrain."

"Winners feel fear, embrace failure and take action anyway.

Winners challenge fear and failure with action every day.

Along the way you will fray.

Some days will be colorful and others will be gray.

Think of the gray day as a straw in the abundance of hay.

You fall, you learn, you get up and you take action anyway.

And you may feel sometimes lonely or even stray.

It is the price that winners pay.

To finally see that golden day.

The day you celebrate, you dance, and you sway,

The day you pray and play,

The day you sing and say,

I felt fear, I embraced failure and I took action anyway.

So, what are you going to do today?"

"I am ready to find my way."

"Hop in, my dear. Success to your brave heart is near."

Aidan signaled with his right arm going up and down twice. Karam's heart and feet danced in excitement to get on board the journey toward happiness, to embrace success.

The audience jumped to their feet to give a standing ovation. Parents held their children. People sat back to think about what had just happened and how they could make the world a better place.

As for Maximus, he stood up and gave Maher a long and warm hug, saying, "You are tremendous, my son."

"It's all thanks to you and to your brilliant ideas. I think the pilot program is beautiful and I think we can make it work for many other people. What do you say?"

"It will be as successful as you want it to be, son. It is yours."

"This is a lot Dad. This is your creation, your program, and I am only a player. I can't take the credit for it. Besides, it is a colossal change from my corporate job and I am not sure if I..."

"Son, it is about the depth of the impact, not its width. It is about the quality of the legacy, not the credit. *It is about what you can, not what you can't*. Are you with me?

For the first time in his life, Maher felt his father asking him for something. He sensed his father's request for help to deliver his message to the universe. He never thought he would be in this position but he felt privileged. His feelings of privilege and empowerment were quickly muddied with worry. He lifted his head to face Maximus' wondering eyes and said:

"This is big, Dad. I don't want to destroy what you have built over decades. What if I disappoint you?"

"Look at what you have done in couple of days. Look at your impact on the children tonight. Look at the waves of emotions you triggered in these parents. These are results, son. Results don't lie. These are your results. Besides, you are the son of Maximus, how bad can you be?" (Smiling)

"I will need your help, Dad. This is the moment. It feels right. It is right. What's a person's value if he doesn't add to the excellence of humanity? I am in. I owe you a rough plan by the time we land in the city tomorrow."

"I can't wait," said Maximus.

Nagnag: Wow... where did that come from? That happened way faster than I could see. Did the idea even cross your mind? How did it bypass me?

Maximus: That's what happens when the stars line up, my good friend.

Nagnag: I like that. I also like how you called me your friend. Why don't we stay that way forever?

Maximus: It is up to you. Be cool and I will be cool. Be the igniter that I need you to be and you will always be pleased with me. How about that?

Nagnag: I am what you want me to be pal. You created me, remember?

Maximus: Right. So here's the deal. As you know, I have been trying to write that book about my grandfather's legacy for the last few days. It has not been that smooth. I keep getting emotional and memories take over most of the time. How about helping me get a real start on that book? I will take the rear seat on the plane tomorrow and we can have all the chat time you need."

Nagnag: You mean the chat time that *you* need?

Maximus:(Smiling.) Yes. You are correct. Let me greet the people before they go home for the night and we'll catch up tomorrow.

Nagnag: And "I am correct"?! This is a promising journey already. Deal, my friend. It is a deal.

⌘ ⌘ ⌘

The Fear and Failure (F&F) principles:

- *Befriend failure.*
- *Challenge fear.*
- *Take action anyway.*
- *Reassess and seek feedback.*

"Dear Grandpa..."

You are a whole. You will never be cloned.
You are the only gift of you in the universe.

It is the last day of the family vacation, the day that Maximus dreads the most. He loves being surrounded by people—especially his family and close friends. Endings remind him of the day he lost his grandfather. He also remembers what his grandfather used to tell him about endings and beginnings: "Endings open space for new beginnings. Endings *are* beginnings; you just need to know what is next."

Maximus woke up a couple of hours before dawn. He gently picked up Manam's cage and left the room in a catwalk motion. He headed toward the beach as he lifted the cage to face Manam and whispered, "Good morning, buddy."

"Tseh... tseh... Goooood morning."

"How are you?"

"Good... tseh... How are you?"

"Wonderful."

Nagnag: Really? Why this early, man?

Maximus: It is never early enough. The day will slip away like sand between the fingers. Besides, this is a new beginning and I would like to salute the departing waves and be there to witness the birth of the virgin waves.

196

Nagnag: Salute the waves? Virgin waves? Birth of waves? While I admire your creativity, I worry about you sometimes.

Maximus: There's a fine line between creativity and abnormality. If I worried about what others define as normal, I would have never been distinguished. I define my norm. Would you agree?

Nagnag: Truth to be told, you have successfully done so. Okay, so now what? Take a break, man. Isn't it time to rest?

Maximus: There you go again. Bouncing between being a Nagnag and an Igniter. What is the theme for the day?

Nagnag: You decide. Since you applied that fancy Gremlin integration technique, years ago, I lost my identity. I used to know why I was created. Now I have to adapt to your desires.

Maximus: Haha, you mean switching you from being a limiting belief to becoming an energy booster? From a Nagnag to an Igniter? Would you rather I keep you as an empowering partner or replace you all at once?

Nagnag: While I would like to challenge your ability to replace me, I am not going to try. I value your partnership more than winning any battle. Besides, you are more determined than a Chinese bamboo tree. So it would be only a matter of time. I will still be me, when *you* let me; I will also honor our agreement to empower and ignite your torch when you need me.

Maximus: Great. Let's enjoy this beginning then. Enjoy the melody that the soft waves sing, the fresh salty fragrance and the enlightening path the departing moon is tracing on the ocean.

Maximus placed Manam's cage on the sandy beach as he sat down. He extended his arms behind his back to lean on the sand with his palms as he stretched his legs. He inhaled as much as he could from the fresh salty breeze, and he swam in his thoughts. A while passed before Maximus smiled, nodded his head few times, then walked a couple of feet to reach the water. He squatted to touch its surface with his palms and whispered, "Thank you for being a lifelong friend. You have always listened attentively to my stories. You never turned your back, no matter what I had to say. You witnessed my ups and downs. You patiently watched my tears. You cleansed my soul and my memory. You gave me all the time I needed to share with you my intimate thoughts and you sometimes offered an opinion—a wet opinion, yet, an awakening one. Thank you for having a boundless heart. Thank you for your countless gifts. Thank you for loving me as much as I love you."

Nagnag: Aren't you glad I am the only one who can hear you? What would anyone think if they heard you talking about the ocean as if it were your best friend?

Maximus: Someone else's opinion does not make me who I am. Be an igniter please. Retire Nagnag and stay with the program. There... do you see the first line of the dawn touching the horizon? That's where the virgin waves are conceived. They are born on the way to the shore. Let's get ready to welcome them with the virgin swim.

As Maximus finished his thoughts, he heard panting and fast footsteps along the shore coming toward him.

Amir: Uncle Maximus, good morning. I am glad I caught you at the perfect moment.

Maximus: Here's the glorious savior of teens. It is nice of you to join your uncle for another virgin swim.

Amir: Of course. Although that's only part of the reason I am here.

Maximus: You got my curiosity up now. What is it?

Amir: I am meeting with a group of five teenagers this morning. I talked to them about the system I am creating for teens. They loved the idea and they want to help. We agreed to meet for a virgin swim. They laughed when they heard the name and I promised that I would explain.

Maximus: And, you want me to do that part?

Amir: It would be nice, since you created it, but I was hoping for more. It would be great if you would offer them few minutes to share your wisdom.

Maximus: Absolutely; but only few minutes. This is your program and you are the man for the show.

Amir: Of course, thank you. There they are coming along the shore. They are truly a fine group of young men.

Maximus: So are you, young man.

After some introductions and pleasantries, Maximus shared with the newcomers the history of the virgin waves, followed by the actual swim. After that, everyone gathered on the shore in a semi-circle facing Maximus, who faced the ocean.

Maximus: Each of us has a phenomenal dream that he wants to achieve. My question to each one of you is, "What is your most valuable asset that will help you turn that dream into a reality?"

The boys looked at each other, looked at Amir, looked at each other again, and then looked at Maximus, hoping he would explain more. Maximus resumed: "You see, what differentiates humans from any other being is the ability to think. Thinking is the creator's gift to you. The creator blessed you so you can become a creator yourself within the environment you choose. Thinking is the most powerful ability that distinguishes winners from the rest. In order to take advantage of this power, you need to care for its container, the brain.

"You may ask, 'How would I care for my brain?' You can start by reading books and articles that help you know who you are, know your strengths and know your areas for improvements—material that helps you master yourself and shows you how you can shape your future. The brain lives in a bigger container, the body. It only makes sense to take care of the bigger container so the brain functions as intended. You vigorously came jogging early this morning and exercise is one of the best ways to care for your body. Another way is to eat right. Your body is made of natural ingredients, nothing processed, so why would you nourish it with processed food? Now the big question is what does your brain and your body represent?"

"They represent... me?" answered one of the teens.

"Absolutely correct. Brilliant young man," replied Maximus as he squatted to draw on the sand with his index finger. He said as he drew a small circle, "This circle represents you brain. We place it in a bigger circle that represents your body. Then place both circles in a bigger circle that represents the whole. That's you."

As he stood back up he went on, "How you care for your brain and your body will ultimately decide how well and how soon you reach your dreams. *You are the source of everything you receive.* Now, I know you may have many 'how to' questions. Amir is an exceptional coach and mentor. I have full confidence you will benefit tremendously from this experience with him. You are already ahead by thinking of helping with this program. Wait and see how far ahead you will be when you are done. Make a positive impact the world can witness. Make melodies the universe can hear. I will celebrate with you your success."

Amir: Thank you, Uncle Maximus. I never get enough of your wisdom. I wish you could stay here forever. I will stop by before you leave today.

Maximus: I would love for you to visit me in the city. Maybe you can bring your new team to one of the workshops. It will be my pleasure to have all of you there.

He shook their hands as he wished them well. He grabbed Manam's cage and headed back to the resort to join his family and friends before departure.

When Maximus arrived at the resort, he found everyone up and running, packing and getting ready to go back home. It wasn't really anyone's desire to go back to the city life. However, it was time to go home so another vacation could be planned.

Flight Capt.: Sir, we are scheduled to leave in few hours. How does that sound to you?

Maximus: You are the captain and it is time when you say it is. Please inform everyone so we can be on time.

Flight Capt.: Yes.

Elektra: How was it, honey?

Maximus: It was phenomenal as always. I had a chance to meet a fine group of teenagers who will make a difference in their world. I still have one thing to get done before we depart. Have you seen Omar yet?

Elektra: Cindy called a half hour ago and she said they were joining us for our "pre-take off breakfast." It is becoming a tradition, I think. They should be here soon.

Maximus: Great. That gives me enough time to write my note to the teacher.

Maximus took a seat at his room's balcony to face the ocean. He smiled as he petted Manam, then took a pen and paper to write:

"My friend, while I wish you were here to enjoy this special time with us, I admire and respect your commitment and dedication to your life purpose. You are the pride of all educators. I bring to you the salute of the island, its virgin waves, its glorious mountains, its endless blue sky, and the humbleness, drive and love of its people. I know you would have loved being part of the pilot program. I also know you would have enjoyed the stories, the camping, the dinners and meeting Omar. In case you are wondering, yes, I am trying to sell you on this vacation next year. I know Manam will do the rest of the work to convince you. I hope you like the new phrases he picked up in the last few days and I hope they make you smile. This is only a note from the island. I am hoping to see you when we all land safely this afternoon. Until then... I pray you maintain health, prosperity and joy for as long as you live. I pray your giving spring never goes dry. I pray you are rewarded with what continuously nourishes your commitment and dedication to raising a better generation."

Elektra rang her food bell one more time, for the last time in this year's family vacation. Everyone gathered around the big table to share yet another distinguished moment in time, a moment that will never have a twin. Most of the conversations were about funny instances that happened during this trip and previous ones.

Another beautiful chapter is added to everyone's life. I hope it is valuable and memorable enough, thought Maximus as the flight captain announced, while he pulled up a chair to join the family, that the jet was ready.

"There's time for everything, and this is the time where you tighten your ties," said Maximus as everyone looked at him. "You might have made new friends, seen new places, created a memorable spot on this island or were even served nicely somewhere in the resort. Make sure you wish your new friend well and hope you may meet them again as long as you have life in you."

"I need to wish my new butterfly well before I go," said Karam. "Aidan, will you go with me?"

"I think we all have memories in that spot so we can all go. Farris, Aban?" said Aidan.

The four of them jumped out of their seats and ran to their destiny as Leila joined them to ensure they would be back on time for takeoff. As everyone stood up to finish their goodbyes, Omar approach Maximus.

Omar: When will we see you next?

Maximus: When you decide it is time (smiling). I would love to see you soon.

Omar: True (smiling). What I meant was all of you here again. This was a heart lifting time for all of us.

Maximus: Before you know it, my friend. I have been trying to make this large family and friends vacation a tradition and it has gained momentum each year.

Omar: Do you think you can make it twice a year?

Maximus: You know my answer. It is possible, as long as everyone's desire is strong enough.

Omar: True. May wisdom never leave your side. May your desire torch remain ignited forever. May God bless you for what you do.

Maximus: May God bless you for who you are.

Omar: You know I don't like these moments but I can't afford not to take you to the runway. Just promise that when you leave the minibus, you don't say or do anything except waving and promising to come back.

Maximus: I will.

As they embraced, Omar whispered, "God bless you, my good friend and keep your heart warm for the warmth you give all of us."

"I am blessed, my good friend, and my heart is warmed by the warmth of yours," said Maximus. They shook hands in the same sequence they have always done and turned to face different directions.

Paaa Pon Papapa Pon... signaled Omar from his minibus, inviting everyone on board. Omar announced as he shut the bus doors, "All on board. Are you ready?"

"Aye, aye, Captain!" answered everyone.

They arrived to the runway on time. Omar opened the door and stood outside the bus to greet them one by one, wishing each a safe flight and a quick return.

"Uncle Omar, I will send you a card with butterflies on your birthday, I promise," said Karam. "I would love that sweetheart," Omar replied, "I will be waiting for it."

"Thank you, uncle, for helping me wake up, for reminding me of the essence of believing, and for who you are," said Leila as she hugged him.

"I am here when you need me. You are my favorite, just don't advertise it to your brothers," said Omar, smiling.

As Maximus stepped out of the bus, heading to the jet door, he turned halfway toward Omar, waved as he promised and he said, "'See you real soon, by God's will."

The flight captain announced takeoff. The jet engines roared, signaling it was time to reach for the open sky, and they launched. The passengers looked out the windows, giving their last greetings to the island, to its people, it waves, and its mountains. They looked down as everything on the ground became smaller and smaller, as they climbed through the white clouds. While almost everyone started preparing for their return to city life, Maximus took his notebook and pen and settled into the last seat of the jet. He wrote:

To the greatest man I met,

To the most honorable man I know,

To the wisest teacher I learned from,

To my beloved grandfather...

He looked outside the window for a few moments as if he was gaining strength to continue what he started. He picked the pen again, stayed still for few minutes then he dropped it on the notebook.

Nagnag: What is it? You always stop here. You have written those four lines hundreds of times before. What is stopping you from continuing?

Maximus: I don't know. I just stop. It is not easy.

Nagnag: What is?

Maximus: You understand I am addressing the man who shaped my life. The man who showed me every source of knowledge I know today. The man who handed me a treasure so valuable that I am afraid I won't give it justice by including it in one book. The one who is not here to correct me if I misrepresent his legacy.

Nagnag: What makes you think you would misrepresent his legacy?

Maximus: I want it presented to the world the same way he handed it to me: pure, raw and rich. I am afraid my thoughts might modify his legacy and take away its purity. I am afraid I may quote him with my own thoughts.

Nagnag: It is truly honorable of you to insist on the integrity of his legacy. How likely is it that the world, nowadays, may connect with his legacy in its raw form?

Maximus: You may have a valid point.

Nagnag: What I know of any legacy is the power of its continuity and the endless value of its message. *You* are his legacy; you continue his teaching and you have been great at it. So what do you think matters the most: the value of the legacy or its original state?

Maximus: Certainly its value. Its integrity is also valuable and it is important for me to maintain it.

Nagnag: Of course, and I am certain you will find more than one way to accomplish that goal.

Maximus: Wow, look at you coaching me. You are acknowledging, validating and even planting the seed.

Nagnag: I learned from the best. I live in the mind of a good coach. He coaches people to achieve their goals every day. He empowers them to *"Create reality so they can live their destiny."*

Maximus: You are ruling today, and I like that. Thank you for your help.

Nagnag: One more thing. You said something about his treasure in one book. What made you think it will be just one book?

Maximus: I like how you think. It's a good possibility. Why not a serious of books? Good brain.

Nagnag: Someone is patting himself on the back. I am proud of you as well. Now how do you feel about going back to writing?

Maximus: Pretty good. I'll try again.

Nagnag: Try?

Maximus: (Smiling.) You're good. Okay, I am going to write now.

Maximus took a deep breath as he pushed his back against his chair to feel his weight; then he looked toward his mother's seat.

Her profile reminded him of his grandfather's profile. He smiled, he picked the pen and resumed his writing:

To the greatest man I met,

To the most honorable man I know,

To the wisest teacher I learned from,

To my beloved grandfather,

I miss you. I miss you more than I can describe. I'd give my life to see you one more time, hold your hand, walk by the river with you and learn one more lesson from you. You blessed me with your time, your experience, your thoughts and your love. You planted in me the value of thinking and the grace of giving. You showered me with your care, attention and desire to excel. You taught me how to lead and follow, how to plan and implement, how to gauge and correct, and how to explore and decide. You handed me the guide to a successful life and I am forever grateful.

In my darkest times I remember the darkness you lived in the mine for years. I also remember how you found your world by believing that six feet of light ahead was enough to reach your goal. You gave me the light that showed me the way all these years.

I write to you today on paper after I wrote to you for tens of years in my memory. I am writing to ask your permission, your blessing and your help. I am asking your permission to take your message and wisdom further than they have reached. I am asking your blessing so I have the courage to bring our memories to life again. I am asking for your help to correct me and remind me when I misquote anything from your teaching. This letter is only the beginning.

Beginnings are the oxygen of life. Ideas are the mind's babies. Starting is the mother of greatness, as you always said.

May every pen stroke in this letter bring you countless blessings.

May you be blessed for every soul who has learned, and will learn, from your wisdom.

May God bless you for what you taught me.

May God give me strength to continue your work.

He laid the pen on the notebook and reached for his grandfather's watch, chained to his jacket pocket. He caressed it, kissed it, put it back in the jacket's tiny pocket by his heart. He placed his palms on his thighs, pushed his back against the seat and relaxed his shoulders. He took a deep breath as he closed his eyes. He smiled, and whispered, "Dream, Wonder, Believe, Own, Plan, Act and take care of *you*. Every moment is a beginning worth pursuing. Every beginning is a chance to nourish life with excellence."

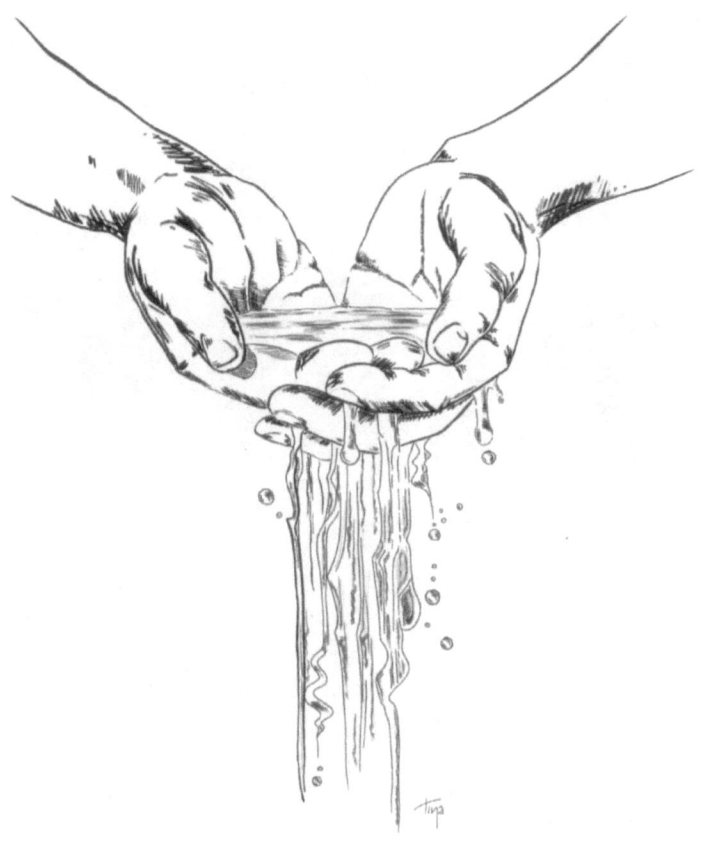

Welcome Back

Here we are at the end of the book and the beginning of your journey. I hope you found the stories inspiring and the lessons valuable. Knowledge is power. Action is winner's attitude. I invite you to continue your quest. You are welcome to start here:

✓ A *FREE full coaching session* that you can schedule **today** at www.SaverWaves.com

✓ **FREE** eWorkBook, weekly articles, educational videos and other coaching resources at www.SaberWaves.com

✓ **15% discount** to future **live events and publications**. Just send us an email. You can find the events list at www.SaberWaves.com/workshops and you will be the first to know and participate in the upcoming book creation.

✓ An **additional 15%** on proven energy and pinnacle performance assessment tools and debrief sessions.

I hope to see your review on www.amazon.com/dp/B019O9AIYK

-Saber Fatnassi-
SaberWaves Coaching
4196 Merchant PLZ
Suite #355
Lake Ridge, VA 22192
www.SaberWaves.com
Support@SaberWaves.com

www.ingramcontent.com/pod-product-compliance
Lightning Source LLC
Chambersburg PA
CBHW022046240626
47154CB00007B/2581